CEO

Cleo Edison Oliver

Playground Millionaire

SUNDEE T. FRAZIER

Illustrations by
Jennifer L. Meyer

Arthur A. Levine Books
An Imprint of Scholastic Inc.

All rights reserved. Published by Arthur A. Levine Books, an imprint of Scholastic Inc., *Publishers since 1920*. SCHOLASTIC, the LANTERN LOGO, and associated logos are trademarks and/or registered trademarks of Scholastic Inc.

The publisher does not have any control over and does not assume any responsibility for author or third-party websites or their content.

No part of this publication may be reproduced, stored in a retrieval system, or transmitted in any form or by any means, electronic, mechanical, photocopying, recording, or otherwise, without written permission of the publisher. For information regarding permission, write to Scholastic Inc., Attention: Permissions Department, 557 Broadway, New York, NY 10012.

This book is a work of fiction. Names, characters, places, and incidents are either the product of the author's imagination or are used fictitiously, and any resemblance to actual persons, living or dead, business establishments, events, or locales is entirely coincidental.

Library of Congress Cataloging-in-Publication Data

Frazier, Sundee Tucker, 1968– author.
  Cleo Edison Oliver, playground millionaire / Sundee T. Frazier ; illustrations by Jennifer L. Meyer.
    pages cm
  Summary: Fifth-grader Cleo Edison Oliver is full of money-making ideas, and her fifth-grade Passion Project is no different — but things get more complicated when she has to keep her business running, be a good listener when her best friend needs her, and deal with the bully teasing her about being adopted at the same time.
  ISBN 978-0-545-82235-0 (hardcover. : alk. paper) 1. Adopted children — Juvenile fiction. 2. African American families — California — Juvenile fiction. 3. Money-making projects for children — Juvenile fiction. 4. Friendship — Juvenile fiction. 5. California — Juvenile fiction. [1. Moneymaking projects — Fiction. 2. Business enterprises — Fiction. 3. Friendship — Fiction. 4. Adoption — Fiction. 5. African Americans — Fiction. 6. California — Fiction.] I. Meyer, Jennifer L., illustrator. II. Title.
  PZ7.F8715Cl 2016
  813.6 — dc23
  [Fic]
                                                                2015015763

10 9 8 7 6 5 4 3 2 1   16 17 18 19 20

Printed in the U.S.A.   113
First edition, February 2016

Book design by Mary Claire Cruz

For Tasha, who is full of great ideas
—with love, DeeDee

Contents

CHAPTER 1

A New Name, a New Business

Cleo wrote her new name in fancy lettering, the curlicue kind she'd learned from Caylee. It didn't look as good as it would have if her best friend had done it, but it would work. She took down the California license-plate door sign that said CLEO'S ROOM and hung her new sign in its place:

cleopatra edison oliver, CEO.

Perfect.

Josh appeared from his and Julian's room. He stared at her door, slurping his Dum-Dum. "Edison's not your middle name."

1

No, it wasn't. Lenore was. But she didn't want that one. Not since Lexie Lewis had gotten ahold of it and started calling her "Le*Snore*."

"It is now." She started into her room.

"But you can't just change your name." *S-s-slurp.* "Can you?"

She turned. Josh ran into her, jabbing her with his dumb Dum-Dum stick.

"Ow!"

"Sorry." *S-s-slurp.*

She rubbed her chest where the stick had poked her. "You can do anything you want with your name. It's *yours*."

Josh sucked thoughtfully, as if this obvious fact had never occurred to him. He followed her across the room. "But Edison is our grandparents' name."

Cleo reached under her bed and pulled out the signs she'd made the night before. "I don't think they'll mind."

"But you'll have two last names!"

"Women with two last names sound more professional."

Josh snorted. "You're not a woman!"

"Well, I *will* be! Now, go away." She grabbed the roll of masking tape from her desk drawer, dropped everything on her royal-purple comforter, and high-stepped onto the bed. She stood eye-to-eye with her poster of Fortune A. Davies.

Fortune had skin that gleamed like a polished chestnut, dazzling white teeth, and a sparkle in her eye that said, "I believe in you!" Her arms were flung wide, forever frozen in an almost-hug. How Cleo wished she could step into the picture and get that hug.

"Why'd you put your initials after your name?"

Cleo turned. The beads at the ends of her freshly braided hair clicked against one another. Josh was staring at her door again.

She jumped down from the bed and grabbed the signs and tape. "Those aren't my initials. I mean, they *are*, now that I've changed my name, but —" She huffed. "Don't you know anything about business, Josh?"

"Not really. Just what you've taught me." He

grinned. He had a huge gap where his bottom two teeth had been.

What would he do without her? "CEO stands for Chief Executive Officer."

Josh's forehead wrinkled. "What's that mean?"

"It's the person in charge of a company."

"Why don't they just call it 'Person In Charge,' then? It's easier to understand."

Cleo rolled her eyes. She started down the stairs.

"But, Cleo, you don't *have* a company."

He had stopped following her. *Finally.*

"I do now! *Cleopatra Enterprises, Inc.*!"

Barkley greeted her at the bottom of the stairs, panting from his "long trek" across the kitchen. His tail slapped the wall. Cleo crouched to get her good-morning kisses. "Ew, Barkley. Not only are you seriously overweight, you've got a bad case of morning breath!"

Barkley barked.

"I think it's this new low-fat dog food we're feeding him," Dad said, scooping kibbles from a ginormous bag of Slim 'N' Trim Canine Sardine Meal. Mom wasn't about to switch dog foods until the whole entire bag was used, and as long as he had to eat that fishy stuff, Barkley's breath was doomed.

Barkley nudged the food with his nose but didn't eat any.

Mom turned from the counter where she was stirring something that looked like sticky birdseed in a bowl. Her T-shirt exposed her formidable arms. Not particularly muscular, but solid. "I don't think he likes it," Mom said, watching Barkley.

"*I* like it!" Julian slid into the room, wearing his Iron Man pajamas.

"What?" Mom's eyes popped wide.

"It's Fish Stick Cap'n Crunch!" Cleo's littlest brother snatched a piece of dog food and crunched it in his mouth. Barkley looked at him quizzically, then took a begrudging bite himself.

"When have you had Cap'n Crunch cereal?" Mom demanded.

"At Damon's house."

"That's the last time I'm letting you go there," Mom said. "That stuff isn't fit for human consumption!"

Julian scowled. The rest of them laughed, even Mom. But then she added, "I'm not joking."

Cleo was tempted to try a bite of fish stick–flavored Cap'n Crunch herself, but she couldn't afford to have stinky breath on her first day of business. "Can I take the card table outside?" she asked.

"Uh-oh. Cleopatra 'I Have an Idea' Oliver is at it again!" Dad winked at her.

"You mean, Cleopatra *Edison* Oliver, CEO."

"Ooo, my daughter, the company president." Dad nodded. "I like the sound of that." Cleo loved her dad, with his crazy, curly, nutty-professor hair. He knew nothing about business, but that didn't keep him from being gung ho about it.

Mom fixed her bright blue eyes on Cleo. "What do you plan to *do* with the table?"

"It's the grand opening of CLEO'S AWESOME AVOCADO STAND!" She held up her signs, then realized they were upside down. She flipped them around.

Dad read aloud. "'Blowout sale!!'? 'Everything must go!!!'?" He looked at her. "On your first day of business?"

"It's advertising, Dad. I'm trying to get people's attention."

"Right . . ."

She produced the sign that said <u>HUGE</u> LABOR DAY SAVINGS!!! "It's all about how you spin things. Marketing is eighty percent of sales, Dad."

"Is that so?"

Mom cut in again. "So what's your plan, exactly?"

"I'm going to sell the avocados from our trees! Barkley's blown up like a balloon from eating too many of them off the ground. And let's be honest, how much more guacamole can we eat?"

"A lot!" Dad said.

Mom's eyes slid to Dad's waistline. Dad scooped up Julian and tickled him all the way to the family room. JayJay shrieked with laughter.

"How much do avocados cost at the store?" Cleo asked.

"Oh, anywhere from a dollar to a dollar fifty apiece. Sometimes as much as two fifty if they're big."

Cleo's heart did a happy dance. The day before, she had counted almost *sixty* avocados on their three trees. And she was going to sell them all!

Josh rushed into the kitchen. "Mom, can we buy my Nerf gun today? *Please??*"

Mom was forming the birdseed goop into balls and plopping them onto a baking sheet. "Do you have half the money yet?"

"No."

"Keep saving!" she sang.

Josh scowled and stomped through the kitchen.

Cleo hurried across the room. "As always, I'll give away ten percent of whatever I make." She looked Mom in the eye. "It's Fortune Principle Number Ten, you know."

"That's wonderful, honey. But for the record, that wasn't her original idea."

"What do you mean?"

"God told us to do the same thing about four thousand years ago."

Oh no. Not another one of Mom's sermons. "What are you making, anyway?"

Mom shoved what looked like lollipop sticks into the balls. Her eyes lit up. "Longevity Lollipops!"

"Longevity?"

"Long life. They're full of stuff that's good for you."

Too bad. Cleo had been about to ask for one. "So can I? Take the card table outside?"

"If you think you can convince people to buy the fruit off our trees, by all means, sell away!"

If she could convince people? "Convince" was practically her middle name!

Except it wasn't. As of today, it was *Edison.* Cleopatra Edison Oliver, CEO. Person In Charge.

CHAPTER 2

May the Sales Force
Be With You™!

Cleo taped her signs to the chain-link fence that surrounded their front yard. Then she stacked avocados in neat pyramids on the table. Product display was a very important part of sales. Grandpa Williams had taught her that. He'd owned his own market until the grocery giant WinCo opened nearby.

She pulled out the cutting board and knife she'd "borrowed" when Mom had left the kitchen to help Julian find something in the boys' bedroom. Grandpa Williams said samples were a must in any quality produce department. *Customers deserve no less!* Plus, they increased sales.

She was all set to sell when Julian and Barkley appeared. Her brother wore his fluorescent green *Star Wars* T-shirt with his orange-brown-and-turquoise plaid shorts. To top it off, he'd chosen his purple-and-gold Lakers kneesocks, each blazoned with a picture of Basketball Hall of Famer Magic Johnson going to the hoop. The outfit was hideous . . . but noticeable. With those clothes and a sign, he'd get *everyone's* attention.

"May the Sales Force be with you!" she said, cracking up at her own joke and making Jay giggle. She just might have to trademark that.

She set her brother on the corner with the sign SAVE OUR DOG!! BUY AVOCADOS!!! and told him to dance. Barkley lay at JayJay's feet, looking very sad and overweight.

People walking by with their dogs, people out jogging, even a few people in cars stopped to ask how buying avocados could save their dog — and then they bought avocados. Sometimes one, sometimes three or four.

Miss Jean from next door tried to trade eggs from her backyard chickens, but Cleo held out for cash. She couldn't bank eggs. Not to mention what would Horizon Home, the shelter for homeless moms and their kids that she gave her ten percent to, do with a bit of egg?

Fred and Pedro came by with their Jack Russell terrier, Bowmore. He and Barkley were good friends. They bought a whole dozen, saying they'd do anything to save Bowmore if *he* were in danger of eating himself to death.

Cleo was at the avocado trees, replenishing her stock, when JayJay started dancing and flinging the sign around again. "Hi, Grandpa Williams!" he yelled. "Want to buy something?"

"What's your sister selling this time?" His friendly voice came from up the street.

"Cleo's Awesome Avocados!" Cleo shouted, rushing back to the table. "Best in all of Altadena Heights!"

The elderly man ambled down the sidewalk, leaning on his redwood walking stick with the dog's-head handle.

"Good morning, Grandpa Williams!" Cleo called, waving and smiling. He wasn't their actual grandpa. They just called him that. She'd been at the Williamses' house the day before, getting her braids redone for the first day of school. Mom hired their granddaughter, Tasha, to do Cleo's hair and sometimes to babysit. Mom had learned a lot of things about African American hair care, but doing tiny cornrow braids wasn't one of them. Her and Cleo's relationship couldn't handle tiny cornrow braids.

"How are my grandkids this fine Labor Day morning?" Mr. Williams asked.

"Great!" Cleo picked up a bag of avocados and held it open for him to see. "Normally, I'd sell these for four dollars. But for you, I'll make it three. Since you're part of my Loyal Customers program."

He peered into the bag. "Am I, now?"

"You've bought from all my businesses."

"Absolutely! Although, I still don't know how you convinced me I needed seven pairs of rainbow-striped toe socks."

"One for every day of the week!"

"Or the dog-leash decorative decals . . . since I don't own a dog."

"You can decorate other things with them."

"But I sure love my knitted coasters! Use 'em all the time."

"They were supposed to be Barbie rugs. But see, you found a perfect way to use those!"

He threw back his head and laughed. "You got it right, there, little sister. I sure did!"

Cleo held up a slice of avocado. "Sample?" She grinned.

His eyes gleamed. "My apprentice has learned well." He took a bite. "That's some fine fruit!" He slipped his hand into his jacket pocket and pulled out three shiny dollar coins — the gold kind that Cleo loved. He gave one to Julian and one to Cleo. "This one is for Brother Joshua," he said, placing the last coin in her hand.

She wanted to say that as president of the company, *she* made the financial decisions, but she couldn't talk back to Grandpa Williams. Plus, Jay had helped. He deserved to be paid. She'd make sure Josh earned his dollar as well.

They said thank you, and then JayJay zoomed off, shouting, "I'm going to show Mom and Dad — I got real gold!"

Grandpa Williams winked at her and gave Barkley's head a pat. "Thanks for the 'Awesome Avocados'!"

"Don't forget to tell everyone you see that we're here," she said.

He raised his cane as he walked away. "Will do. Keep up the good work!"

Cleo was at the table, counting her money, when Josh came around the corner with his bin of DinoFormers. His LA Dodgers cap snugged his curly hair, as usual. The hat, a gift from his and JayJay's first mom, Melanie, never left his head when he was outdoors.

"Twenty-eight, twenty-nine . . . ," Cleo counted.

Josh's eyes got huge when he saw her pile of dollar bills. "Whoa! You made all that money?"

"Uh-huh. And there's plenty more where this came from!" She motioned to the trees in their yard. At least another thirty dollars hung on the branches.

Barkley hobbled over. Cleo kissed the top of the dog's head. "Thanks for getting fat, Barks. I might never have realized what a gold mine I was sitting on." She held up an avocado. "*Green* gold!"

Josh set down his toy bin. Barkley stuck his nose into it and sniffed around. "No, Barkley!" Josh pushed the dog's head away.

Cleo finished counting the dollar bills. All thirty-three of them. This was the quickest and easiest money she'd ever made from a business. She'd sold plant bulbs (Mom hadn't been too happy when she'd found out Cleo had dug them up from her flower beds), hand-drawn tattoos, God's Eyes, and rides on her Slip'N Slide. Plus, products from a catalog (like tins of popcorn and the toe socks), decorative decals (which could be used for dog leashes *or* other things), and Barbie rugs. But nothing had come close to generating this kind of dough! She couldn't believe this amazing business opportunity had been right in front of her face this whole time and she'd missed it. Avocados just seemed so . . . well, avocado-y. Bland and unexciting and not a very attractive color of green. But people wanted them!

"Speaking of gold, help me sell and I'll give you this dollar." She held up the coin from Grandpa Williams.

He held out his hand. "That's mine already. JayJay told me."

Her shoulders drooped. "Okay." She dropped the coin into his palm, then perked up again. "Help me sell and I'll give you twenty-five cents a bag!" She was feeling generous . . . and she didn't want to be alone.

"That's not very much." Josh crossed his arms and narrowed his eyes.

"I've already sold ten bags. Ten more and you'll have two dollars and fifty cents — three fifty with Grandpa Williams's money — to put toward that Nerf gun."

"What do I have to do?"

"Here." She held out the SAVE OUR DOG!! BUY AVO-CADOS!!! sign. "Just dance around on the corner, like the Pizza-Sign Guy on Lake Avenue." The Pizza-Sign Guy was a real professional. He could do two complete spins while his sign was up in the air.

"No way. Too embarrassing."

She shrugged. "Fine by me."

A silver SUV chugged up the street. Cleo ran to the curb, waving the sign. "Best avocados in all of Altadena Heights! Cheaper than the store! Great guacamole!"

The SUV drove past without slowing. Oh well. She'd get the next one. She turned back to the table. Josh held up Mom's knife by its handle.

"Mom doesn't let you use this knife."

It was true. The fancy Global Chef!® knife Mom had bought from the infomercial was off-limits.

"How do you know?"

"Because I heard her tell you you couldn't."

"That was a long time ago."

"No it wasn't."

"Well, maybe she changed her mind."

"I'm telling her you took her knife."

"No, Josh!"

He started toward the gate.

She dropped the sign and rushed after him. He walked faster. She had to be careful — he was holding a sharp knife, after all. Barkley barked but didn't try to keep up with them.

"I'll give you another dollar. Just let me have it, Josh."

He fumbled with the gate latch. "You're going to be in *b-i-i-i-g* trouble."

The little termite! Why did he always have to ruin everything? She snatched his hat and bolted.

"Give it back!" he shouted. The knife clattered on the sidewalk. Barkley barked louder.

Cleo couldn't afford to look back or worry about the knife now. She gripped her flip-flops with her toes and ran for her life. If Josh caught her, there was no telling what he'd do. He may only have been six to her ten, but he was strong. Much stronger when he was mad.

Josh sprinted behind her, screaming, past Miss Jean's house, past the Williamses', almost to Caylee's before she faked one way and went the other, barely escaping his grasp. She squealed at the thrill of almost getting caught, then giggled.

"It's not funny!" Josh howled.

Cleo turned tail and sprinted for home. Her only hope was to throw the hat at the last second, like a steak to a lion, and make a dash for her bedroom.

"You're mean! I hate you!" Her brother was going berserk.

Cleo's conscience pricked her into glancing back. Suddenly, she was stumbling over the bin of DinoFormers. She yelped and threw the hat at Josh, barely avoiding a crash landing. The cap bounced off his body. He crushed it underfoot as he plowed into her, sending her into the fence. The chain links rattled as he pummeled her. Barkley was also going berserk.

"Stop, Josh! I gave it back!" She covered her face with her hands. The best she could do now was to protect herself from his fists.

The screen door slammed open. "Joshua Myron!" Mom called. In a moment, she was there, prying him off. She wrapped her arms around him and held him like a human straitjacket. "Shhhh. Calm down."

Her brother wheezed. Mom stuck his inhaler in his mouth. "Breathe, Josh." He drew in a deep breath. His brown cheeks were tear-streaked. His upper lip was wet with snot. "You can't do that, Josh. You can't hit when you're angry." Mom stroked his arm.

"She took my hat," Josh said fiercely.

The hat sat crumpled on the ground.

"You took his hat?" Mom's voice was as sharp as her Global Chef!® knife. Her blue eyes pierced Cleo.

The horribleness of the trouble she was in crashed on her like a Zuma Beach wave. Josh's hat was *never* to be taken from his head. It was practically the Eleventh Commandment in their house. She stood and picked up the dented cap. "Here, Josh."

He pulled the hat down on his head, shooting her a fiery look. Then he picked up his bin of toys and stomped toward the gate like a gigantic DinoFormer. Cleo held her breath, expecting him to say something about the knife.

The knife. Barkley sniffed at it where it lay on the sidewalk. If he stayed right there, maybe Mom wouldn't see it.

"*Why,* Cleo? Why are you always pushing the limits? You *know* the hat is out of bounds."

"He started it."

"It doesn't matter! You don't take off his hat!" Mom stared at her disapprovingly. "I expect a serious apology from you."

"Sorry, Josh!" she called to his back.

"No!" Mom's hands flew up in frustration. "A *genuine* apology after thinking about what you've done for an hour in your room."

"What about my business?" She looked at the small pile of avocados still needing to be sold, at her signs hanging on the chain-link fence.

"It can wait. Push everything against the fence and let's go."

Cleo dragged the table toward the fence. She wished she had the power to make things disappear, thinking mostly about the knife, but a little about her brother. Why did he have to be such a baby? What did he think would happen if he didn't wear that raggedy hat outside — the sky would fall on his head? At least he had a birth mom who sent him presents.

Cleo picked up her money container. Maybe if she distracted her mom, she wouldn't notice the knife. "Mom! Guess what? I made thirty-three dollars!"

Mom's eyes widened. "Wow!" For a moment, she looked genuinely impressed, but her Tough Mom face quickly returned. "Now, inside."

Cleo glanced to where the knife *had* been. Barkley lay on the ground with it between his teeth, gnawing on the handle! "No, Barkley! Drop it!" Fortunately, he obeyed.

Mom stared, open-mouthed, at the knife. "What is *that* doing out here?" she said, fists on hips.

Triple fudge and Frigidaire.

Cleo rushed over and picked up the knife. "Mom, listen. I had a great idea! *Samples!*"

Mom was waiting — *wanting* — to be persuaded. "People can't resist samples, Mom. Did you know that samples increase sales by twenty-eight percent?" Cleo didn't know that for sure, but it sounded about right.

Mom crossed her arms. Blinked.

Cleo held up the money container again. "I can make more. Lots more!"

Mom shook her head, looking seriously disappointed in her one and only daughter. "Cleo, I don't really care about the money. I care that you took what wasn't yours without asking. *Twice.*"

Cleo's shoulders drooped. The container hung at her side. "I needed it to cut the avocados."

"You're not allowed to cut with it. You know that too. It's a very sharp knife, Cleo. The sharpest one I have. It's also my *best* knife — not to be flung around outside or chewed on by the dog!" She held out her hand. Cleo gave her the knife.

"But I'm almost eleven. I can handle it!"

"*You* don't decide that."

"I was careful. I didn't hurt myself."

"I'm glad, but that's not the point." Mom sighed. "I'm sorry, Cleo, but you pushed too far this time. Business is over. You're done for the day."

Fortune A. Davies

CHAPTER 3
Telling Fortune

Cleo lay on her bed, fuming. *Apple, Apple, Apple!* (A great made-up swear because it was both a food item *and* a company.) She was so mad she could scream, but that would just get her even more time in her room. *Solitary confinement.* The worst punishment *ever*.

Not only could she not leave her room for an hour, there would be no television for the rest of the day. She would miss *Fortune*! She pounded her mattress and stomped her feet, keeping her voice to a low growl.

She thought about finding Mom and begging for another chance, but that *definitely* would get her more time. Once Mom announced a consequence, she never went back on it. Dad, Cleo could talk into a more reasonable position. But not Mom. She was as immovable as a corporate boss in a labor dispute.

Fortune smiled down from the wall. Fortune — always beaming, always believing, always reminding her she could be the success she wanted to be. Fortune wouldn't have punished her by taking away a whole *day* of doing business. She probably would agree that Josh needed to toughen up a little. And that Cleo was responsible enough to use a chef's knife.

She stood on her bed and looked into Fortune's face, searching again for hints of herself. Brown eyes; long, straight nose; rich brown skin. Cleo had brown eyes, but they weren't as round as Fortune's. Cleo had a long, straight nose, but hers didn't flare out as wide at the bottom. Cleo's skin was brown too, but not nearly as shimmery. Fortune glowed.

The biggest likeness was in their smiles. They both had giant, sparkling smiles that could win people over in an instant. Unless that person was Cleo's mom. Why didn't Mom believe in her like Fortune did? Well, like Fortune *would* if they ever actually met.

She plopped back down on her bed and fell over, her head on her satin-covered pillow. If only she could talk to Fortune.

She sat up straight. Of course! She could write Fortune a *letter*! A well-written letter would get her attention better than an email any day. And if anyone knew how to write a persuasive letter, Cleo did.

She opened her desk drawer and pulled out a piece of the personalized stationery she'd made that weekend, after officially changing her middle name. She looked up Fortune's office address in an issue of *Fortune Women* magazine, then sat down to write.

It took her four drafts and a lot of personalized stationery, but finally it said exactly what she wanted it to say. *Perfect.*

$$$CEO$$$
Cleopatra Edison Oliver, CEO
CLEOPATRA ENTERPRISES, INC.
818 Camphor Street
Altadena Heights, CA 91120

Fortune A. Davies, CEO
Fortune Enterprises, Inc.
150 Madison Avenue
New York, NY 10016

Dear Ms. Fortune A. Davies:

My name is Cleopatra Edison Oliver, I am in the 5th grade, and I am most likely your biggest fan in the WHOLE WIDE WORLD!!! I have been watching Fortune with my mom since I was three years old. Seeing you on TV is actually my VERY FIRST memory! Can any other fan say that?!

Ms. Davies, you talk about purpose a lot. You say yours is "Delivering Destinies and Financing Futures." I have a future in business. I <u>know</u> I do. First of all, there is my name, which I got from my birth mom. (Is it true that you find the pharaohs of Egypt fascinating?) Personally, I LOVE my name because Cleopatra was a very powerful woman (just like you!). Not only am I named after a queen and ruler, but my initials are CEO, <u>and</u> I'm a Capricorn (just like you!), the zodiac's top business achievers. So, Ms. Davies, as you can clearly see, ruling companies is my destiny!

I have tons of ideas for what I will do with the money I make, starting with a special theme park for adopted kids and their families. If I had a dollar for every time my parents said I'd rule the house if they let me, I'd be rich already! But clearly, I am not in charge yet. Today I got in trouble for something, and my mom took away my business for a <u>whole</u> day. Did you ever feel like your parents didn't understand you? What did you do?

I am currently the president and CEO of my very own company, Cleopatra Enterprises, Inc. (I hope you don't mind that it sounds sort of like Fortune Enterprises, Inc.) I have had many product lines over the years, but right now I am focused on avocados. I always give away ten percent of what I make, just like you say in Fortune Principle Number Ten.

This past spring I learned all about what it means to be a CEO when I did a report on "the most influential person in your life." I chose YOU, of course! I am a member of your Fortune's Kids Club and have written to you many times through your website. Your replies have told me to keep watching because you might read my message on your show, and I have — every day at 4 o'clock! You haven't read any of mine on TV yet, but that's okay. I am confident you will very soon!

I know you are SUPER busy running all your businesses, starting schools in other countries, and being on TV, but if you could write me back with the answer to just one very important question, it would make me so excited and happy. I would take your letter to school and show it to EVERYONE. I would frame your letter and hang it on my wall FOREVER. ☺ ☺ ☺ And this is my question: What is the most important thing to do when you're my age if you want to be a huge success like Fortune A. Davies???

Ms. Davies, if you are ever in Los Angeles, I hope you will stop by CLEO'S AWESOME AVOCADO STAND ("The best avocados in all of Altadena Heights!"). You will get a bag of my best avocados — on the house, of course!

Your biggest fan — if I had a million dollars (and one day I will) I'd bet on it,

Cleopatra Edison Oliver

Cleopatra Edison Oliver, CEO (the next Fortune A. Davies!!!)

P.S. I have memorized all ten Fortune Principles for How to Build Your Business and Live the Life You Want. Thanks for all the great advice!

P.P.S. PLEASE, <u>PLEASE</u> write back!!!

She'd come close to adding a P.P.P.S.: "Is there any possible way you had a daughter ten years and eight months ago and that I could be her?" But no. She didn't want to sound desperate. Or pitiful. She was a Very Enterprising Young Lady™. She was on her way to the top! She was going to be a stunning success!!! And now Fortune would know it too.

Thud! The floor shook.

One of her brothers yelled.

Thud!

Josh and Julian were playing paratroopers off the top bunk again. Cleo looked out her window. Mom and Dad were talking in the driveway. Dad clasped his large hands on top of his head. Mom's mouth moved quickly. Her eyebrows pinched together, whether in anger or worry, Cleo couldn't say. Knowing her mom, probably both.

Cleo pounded on the wall between her and her brothers' rooms. "Knock it off, Josh and Jay! You know you're not supposed to be doing that!" They screamed and jumped again.

Thud! Thud!

Cleo yanked open the window, ready to tell on her brothers.

"It's not enough," she heard Mom say. "Our monthly payment is about to go up."

They were talking about it again. *Money.* Mom hadn't worked for the past several years, since they'd gotten the boys.

Dad said something, but his voice was too low to hear. They started walking toward the house. Cleo pulled back so they wouldn't see her. Mom's voice floated up from below. "I'm *not* being too harsh, Charlie. She has to learn that she can't just take whatever she wants whenever she wants it. Do you want to raise a selfish kid?"

Cleo's chest squeezed. She felt hot all over. And something else . . . she didn't know the word for it.

Bad.

She just felt bad. *Full* of badness. She was too selfish for them.

She went to her closet and took down the small

metal safe where she kept her money between trips to the bank. She turned the dial and pulled out ten of the dollars she'd made before screwing up and losing her business for the day.

She took out another piece of stationery, wrote, "So you can buy your Nerf gun. I'm <u>really</u> sorry ☹☹☹" in her best handwriting. She stashed the money and note in an envelope, wrote "Josh" across the front, and quickly slipped it under her brothers' door.

A minute later, Josh bounded in and hugged her so hard he almost made her cry. Dumb kid.

CHAPTER 4
Peanut Butter and Jelly

Cleo woke up Tuesday feeling bearish, which was what you were when things were not looking up. She was intrigued by the thought of getting to know her new teacher, since everyone said he was the *opposite* of his name — Mr. Boring — but she was not really looking forward to school.

First of all, there was the school part. Cleo liked learning things. If only she didn't have to do all those pesky assignments . . .

And *this* year she had to face the awful-est of awful

assignments. The one she'd been dreading since third grade.

The Fifth-Grade FAMILY TREE PROJECT.

Ugh.

Every year, they hung in the fifth-grade hallway of New Heights Elementary — construction-paper trees with green leaves labeled with names. Names of kids' parents, grandparents, great-grandparents, aunts, and uncles. Biological family. Learning about GENES. Finding out about WHERE YOU CAME FROM. All stuff she couldn't do, because her birth parents — *whoever* they were — hadn't wanted her to *know* who they were. She glanced at Fortune A. Davies on her wall.

A knock came at the door. She sat up and put her feet on the floor. Dad poked his head in. "See you later, Sunshine." He came over and kissed the sleep cap that covered her hair. "Have a great first day."

"You're leaving?"

"I told you last night — I've got zero period this year."

"What about chocolate chip pancakes?" They

always had chocolate chip pancakes on the first day of school.

"Rain check. Saturday. Promise." He held out his hand for their special promise handshake: clasp, slide palms, fluttery fingertips. She did it, but not happily. Her day hadn't needed any help getting worse.

Shouting erupted on the other side of the wall. JayJay screamed, then started crying. Footsteps pounded down the hall. "Mo-om! Julian drew on my Nerf gun!"

"Sounds like trouble in paradise. Better go help out." Dad gave her a squeeze. "That was a really generous thing you did, giving your brother that money." Dad had bought the Nerf gun with Josh the night before. They'd gotten a great Labor Day deal, of course.

Cleo let herself be hugged. She inhaled Dad's fresh, just-showered morning scent. Too quickly, he was leaving.

Mom and Dad pecked lips as they crossed paths in the doorway. "See ya after soccer practice," Dad said.

"Cleo, you should be up and dressed by now. What's the holdup?" Mom rushed back out. "Stop hitting your brother with that!"

Cleo pulled herself out of bed and trudged to the closet, took off her purple satin cap, and shook out her braids. She had begged Mom to let her sport the twist-n-curl style Tasha had done for her a few weeks back, but Mom insisted it was too high-maintenance, and it would only last a few days instead of a few weeks. They were sticking with braids . . . for now.

She deliberated for a long time over what to wear. Finally, she decided on her favorite purple-and-orange striped blouse with the ruffles on the cuffs and down the front, even though it was getting a little tight. On the bottom, she wore her black skirt with orange leggings. Her skin peeked through a small hole in one knee, but she didn't think it was too noticeable.

Wear bold. BE bold. It was one of Fortune's favorite sayings. She looked back at the poster. Fortune looked straight ahead, her smile unflinching.

Cleo stood on her bed. She basked in the gaze of the woman's steady, sparkling eyes. Studied her brilliant, poster-perfect smile.

Style. Self-assurance. Success. One day, Cleo would have these things too.

She jumped from the bed and headed to the bathroom.

"No! No! Don't, Mom! Ow! Ow!" Josh jiggled on the bathroom step stool. Mom bent over him with a determined look on her face. She clenched his toothbrush in her fist.

"Josh. Stop wiggling. We have to brush your teeth. *All* of them."

Cleo put toothpaste on her brush. "You should just yank it out, Mom. We could do it while he's sleeping."

Josh narrowed his eyes at Cleo and held up his fist. "I'll give you a knuckle sandwich!"

Mom sighed in frustration. "I wish your uncle hadn't taught you that." She moved in with the brush again. Josh wailed.

"It's just a *tooth*, Josh. You don't have to have a nuclear meltdown over it." Cleo rolled her eyes and started brushing. You would've thought they were threatening to cut off his leg the way he screamed and carried on whenever the subject of pulling his tooth came up.

Finally, they were done. Josh gave Cleo the Evil Eye on his way out the door. "Dear Lord," Mom sighed. "I can't go through this seventeen more times. And I'm definitely *not* doing what I did the first time. Ever. Again."

Josh had held out so long with his first loose tooth that, by the end, it was hanging by a mere *thread* of gum tissue. He had swallowed it in his sleep, which meant that if Mom wanted to have Josh's first lost tooth in her special memories box she'd have to dig through the toilet for it.

Which she did. Every time he pooped. Eventually, they found it.

No keepsake, no matter how precious, was worth that.

Cleo finished brushing her teeth, then grabbed her letter to Fortune and ran to the mailbox. She put the letter inside and raised the little red flag.

In four to five days, according to Mom, it would be delivered to Fortune's office. She would read it and see how determined Cleo was to succeed. She would write back and sign the letter with her very own hand.

Cleo headed back to the house, pondering Fortune's response. A letter from Fortune signed in ink from a pen she had held. It would practically be the same as being in the woman's presence, having her signature like that. It would hold magic. It would be Cleo's most prized possession ever.

In fact, she probably would . . . yes, she'd even stick her hand in a toilet to save it.

As the family minivan pulled up to school, Cleo searched the huddles of kids, looking for Caylee's black hair and baby-blue suede jacket. Cleo hadn't seen her best friend in *ten* whole days. She'd been visiting her dad at his new house in Palm Springs.

Mom came around to the side door. She hugged Josh hard and kissed his face before he jumped down. "Have a great day, my big first-grader!"

Cleo stepped out and Mom wrapped her arms around her. "Love you, kiddo." She kissed her forehead. "You sure you don't want me to hang around until the bell rings?"

"I'm *sure*."

"You nervous?"

"*No-o*." Why would she be nervous?

"You were clicking your wrist."

Cleo's right wrist had a click in it. She had a habit of circling it until she heard seven clicks in a row, for good luck. Maybe she did it a bit more when she was nervous. "I'm okay."

"Come on!" Josh said urgently. "Benny is waiting for me!"

Mom squeezed her again. "See you after school, love."

"Okay. Love you too."

They walked toward the building. Josh turned and waved as the van pulled away.

"Remember, I'm in Room Fourteen if you need me," Cleo said when Mom was gone.

"Why would I need you?" He peered out from beneath his Dodgers hat.

So much for trying to be a helpful big sister. "I don't know. What if you get a bloody nose?"

"I'll pinch it and go see Nurse Bishara." Between nosebleeds, tummy aches, and his asthma, Josh spent a fair amount of time in the nurse's office. He and Nurse Bishara were practically best buds.

She shrugged. "Okay."

Josh saw Benny and took off running.

"See you later!" she called.

"Bye!"

She kept going, through the front doors and the short hallway that separated the multipurpose room and gym from the main office, and onto the playground. Caylee was walking up at the same time from the opposite direction. "Peanut butter!"

"Jelly!"

Their fourth-grade teacher, Mrs. Nuesmeyer, had told them they were like peanut butter and jelly — impossible to separate.

Cleo ran and gave Caylee a huger-than-normal Bug-a-Hug, as if they'd been apart for months. (A Bug-a-Hug was a hug they'd invented that was so tight it practically made your eyes bug out.)

"Nice outfit!" Cleo stood back so she could admire Caylee's clothes.

Her turquoise T-shirt came down over the hips of her cuffed jeans, which had hearts and flowers stitched on the legs. Over her shirt, she had on a totally adorable purple bolero sweater. And on her feet, purple Mary Jane shoes.

"My dad took me back-to-school shopping."

Cleo's striped, too-tight, button-up blouse suddenly seemed faded. The sleeves felt a little too short and the hole in her leggings felt gaping. Her family hadn't gone back-to-school shopping this year.

Caylee's chin-length, straight black hair was held back on either side by funky felt hair clips — a paintbrush on one side and an artist's palette on the other.

"Did he buy you these cool clips too?" Cleo reached out to touch the palette.

"I made them, actually."

Cleo's eyes bugged without the hug. "Wow! They're great! You could sell these."

"Thanks." Caylee slipped her arm through Cleo's and they walked toward the painted line on the playground outside their classroom. They reached their door — the only ones in line.

"Where were you last night? I sent Barkley over."

Last spring, when she'd been grounded from the phone for a month for calling an 888 fortune-teller number, she had created a message capsule that attached to her dog's collar with Velcro — Cleo's Canine Carrier Capsule™. Then she trained Barkley to take messages back and forth between the Ortegas' and her house, and — *voilà!* — Barkley the Carrier Dog! The night before, he'd come back with her message still in the capsule.

"I got home late from my dad's."

"Did you swim? I can't wait to go with you. I'd be in the pool the whole time!"

Caylee looked at her feet. She was suddenly very quiet. "I didn't really feel like swimming." She kept her head down for so long that Cleo looked too, thinking maybe she'd seen something interesting like an un-chewed piece of bubblegum or a lost earring. "He's got this new girlfriend . . . They were always going off places and leaving me and E.J. behind."

The whistle to line up shrilled.

A *girlfriend*? Something just didn't seem right about a dad having a girlfriend.

Cleo was about to say so when she heard Lexie Lewis's mocking voice. "Hey, LeSnore, how was your summer? Much more Le*Boring* than mine, I'm sure."

Cleo stood as straight and tall as she could, but Lexie still looked down on her. She wore a fur-lined, hooded vest. A gold purse covered in rhinestone flowers hung by her side. Who brought a purse to school? Lexie Lewis, that's who.

"I see you're still wearing braids." Lexie's hair was pressed and sleek, all the way down to her shoulders.

"I see you're still at New Heights."

Lexie always bragged that her parents planned to put her and her brother, Cole, in private school. *If only they would*, Cleo thought. Her life would be so much easier.

"Did you think I wouldn't be?"

Hoped was more like it. "What about private school?"

"We're applying for middle schools now. Elementary doesn't really matter, anyway." Her eyelids fluttered. "How are your dolls?"

Cleo clenched her teeth. "I don't play with dolls."

"You did last year."

"Well, I don't anymore. I'm too busy running my businesses."

"Oh, like selling *doll* rugs?"

"No. Avocados."

Lexie sputtered. "Avocados?"

"Yep. Made thirty-three dollars yesterday."

"Wow, Cleo," Caylee said. "That's a lot!"

Cleo could tell Lexie didn't want to look too impressed. "Not nearly enough to buy *this*." She held up the purse. "If you're wondering, yes, it's a *real* Trudy Ferretti." She admired her own handbag.

"Tooty-Fruity?" Caylee said, her nose wrinkled. "Isn't that an ice cream flavor?"

Cleo cracked up.

Lexie Lewis just cracked. At least it looked like her long, skinny face had. "I said, '*Trudy Ferretti*.' But, of course, you two wouldn't know."

Cleo knew, actually. Fortune loved Trudy Ferretti shoes and handbags.

"She's only the hottest designer of the decade!" Lexie crowed.

The whistle sounded again. "Too bad we're not in the same class this year, LeSnore. I could have taught you some things about fashion." She looked Cleo up and down. "I'll give you a quick tip now. Get rid of the religious leggings."

Cleo looked at her, confused. *Religious leggings?*

Lexie pointed at Cleo's knee. "They're *holey*." She laughed. As if she were funny.

Cleo stuffed her fists into the crooks of her arms and made her eyes into slits. If Lexie Lewis wasn't careful she was going to get herself a knuckle sandwich before this year was over.

"See you around!" The Tooty-Fruity purse swung out to the side as she swiveled and flounced toward the other fifth-grade line.

"For your information, my middle name isn't Lenore anymore!" Cleo called after her. "It's *Edison!*"

Lexie ignored her.

"She's *horriful*," Caylee said, using one of their favorite made-up words. The opposite of *horriful* was *splendarvelous*.

They both giggled, and Cleo's fists relaxed. The door to their classroom opened and a tall, skinny man in a red-blue-and-green Hawaiian shirt came out. "Hello, Room Number Fourteen Fifth-Graders! Do I have some big plans for *you!*" He high-fived Cleo, Caylee, and a few other kids at the front of the line.

Cleo wished she had some big plans for how to deal with Lexie Lewis. She glanced at Lexie's purse, glinting in the sun, and told herself she could care less if Lexie Lewis owned a Trudy Ferretti — even if the designer label *was* Fortune's favorite.

CHAPTER 5

The Name Game

C leo found her desk close to the door they'd just come in. It was pulled together with three others, same as all the desks in the room. She checked the folded-paper name tents in her group.

Nuts and Nintendo! Caylee wasn't one of her table buddies.

Instead, Cleo would be sitting next to none other than Cole Lewis, Mr. BMOC — Big Man of the Classroom. Cole was working the room, giving fancy handshakes and fist bumps to his buddies. Everyone loved Cole . . . including Caylee. Cleo was not as impressed. The fact that he was Lexie Lewis's twin probably didn't help.

Caylee was one table over, on the other side of where Cole *would* be, when he finally stopped chatting it up. Caylee was changing her first name from MICHAELA to CAYLEE on her name tent. She and Cleo had come up with the nickname in second grade so that they could have the same first and last initials.

Cleo grabbed her name tent, pulled her favorite purple pen from her backpack, and wrote EDISON in cramped, sloping letters between CLEOPATRA and OLIVER. Then she added a comma and CEO to the end.

Lucky Caylee . . . she was sitting across from sophisticated and stylish Amelie Martinet, a girl with beautiful, long, reddish-brown hair who spoke three languages and whose family vacationed in faraway places like France and the Cape Verde Islands. Sitting across from Cleo was Micah Mitchell, who had a reputation for armpit-farting and breaking into song at totally inappropriate times.

The fourth seat belonged to Anusha Chatterjee. With that last name, you might have thought she was born to talk (like Cole Lewis apparently had been), but she was the quietest girl in the whole school. Cleo would bring her out of her shell. That's probably why Mr. Boring had put them together.

"Hi, Anusha! Did you have a good summer?"

"Yes." Anusha bent over to put her things in her desk, and that was the end of the conversation. Ah well. All worthy projects took time.

Cole's rear end finally made touchdown. He reached out and nudged Cleo's arm. "Hey, Cleo. What's up?"

"Fortune Enterprises stock," she said with satisfaction. She had looked online that morning. One day soon, she would be a shareholder herself.

Cole gave her a funny look. He turned to Micah. "How you doin', table buddy?" They slapped a high five.

You can think I'm strange all you want, Cole Lewis. I'll be laughing all the way to the bank.

Mr. Boring blew into a small wooden thing. It looked like the carved handle of a crank, or the top of a candlestick, but it quacked like a duck! *Quack! Quack-quack!* The ridiculous sound definitely got their attention. It also made everyone laugh. Cleo liked Mr. Boring already.

Once everyone quieted down, Mr. Boring did not do the usual *boring* thing of calling roll. Instead, he announced in a TV game show voice, "It's time for The Name Game!" Cleo felt a rush of energy. She *loved* games.

In The Name Game, each person would have a turn to tell the rest of the class about his or her name: where it came from, what it meant, why their parents chose it. The one rule was that there were to be no interruptions while the person was sharing. And absolutely *no* poking fun.

If a person *did* interrupt, Mr. Boring's Three Strikes and You're IN policy would take effect.

"Three strikes and you'll be *inside* for recess. And there's no way you want to spend your recess with me.

My name *is* Mr. *Boring,* after all." His eyes roamed the room. He was serious, but clearly *not* boring.

Then he made them all raise their right hands and swear on their parents' good reputations that they would not interrupt — no way, no how.

"No way, no how!" they repeated enthusiastically.

"Now that we have the formalities out of the way, let's . . . *play the game!*"

Cleo was disappointed that this game didn't have a winner, and even more disappointed when Mr. Boring started on the opposite side of the room — she was bursting with things to say! — but still, it would be fun to learn about people's names and how they got them. More fun than doing some time-wasting *assignment,* that was for sure. She listened, more or less, to her classmates, all the while crafting what she would say about herself.

Steffy Lee had been named after the midwife who delivered her. Tessa Hutchfield was named after her grandma. Amelie's parents had just liked the sound of the name — it was musical — which was fitting, because so was Amelie. She had the best singing voice of anyone at New Heights Elementary.

Caylee — Michaela — had been named after an archangel!

"Is an archangel like an archenemy?" Quentin McDonnell asked. He'd gotten his name, which meant *five*, from being the fifth kid in his family.

"Not exactly," Mr. Boring said. "Although they have this *prefix* in common, don't they?" He wrote the words on the board and underlined the *arch* part on both. "*Arch* means *chief*, so an archangel would be top dog in a company of angels. And an archenemy would be someone's chief nemesis — his or her number one enemy."

Cleo imagined Lexie Lewis's smug face.

Caylee, on the other hand, had been her arch-*friend* since second grade. How had Cleo never known that her best friend was named after the top dog of a company?! No wonder they had always gotten along so well.

Finally, they got to Cleo's table. Cleo was about to raise her hand, but Mr. Boring called on Anusha first. She spoke so quietly Mr. Boring had to ask her to repeat herself. Her name came from an Indian word that meant *beautiful morning star.* Everyone thought that was really cool.

Cleo wondered if *her* name had a meaning. She'd have to look into that. She started to raise her hand again, but Cole got to go next. She had had butterflies in her stomach earlier, but not anymore. Now she had *bats.* This waiting was killing her!

Cole was named after a famous singer, Nat King Cole. He started impersonating the man's singing. "'Unforgettable, that's what you are . . .'" He was *so* cheesy. Cleo looked at Caylee, planning to roll her eyes, but Caylee's gaze was fixed on the singing fool. Why did her face look so dreamy? *Oh, Caylee.*

Mr. Boring asked Cole if his twin sister was also named after someone famous.

"She's named after a car." Cole snickered. "Our mom always wanted to have a Lexus. *Alexis.* Get it?" Now he laughed loud, like a donkey. Maybe Cole Lewis wasn't so bad, after all — if he could laugh at his sister.

Hmmm . . . Lexie Lewis had been named after a car. Cleo would keep the info in her back pocket . . . just in case.

Finally, Mr. Boring called on her. "And how about you, *Cleopatra?*" She liked the way he said her name, long and drawn out, with a trill on the *r*, like an actor in one of those Shakespeare plays. "I'm extremely curious to know how you got your intriguing name."

Intriguing! He hadn't called any of the *other* kids' names that.

Cleo's heart hammered. Her mouth went dry. She was still eager to share, but she was also crazy nervous, she realized. "I got it from my birth mom," she began proudly.

"Your *what?*" It was Rowdy Jimmy Ryerson.

Mr. Boring made a whistling sound and held up his hands in a *T*.

"Time out," he said. "Jimmy, that's Strike One." Jimmy's name was the first to go on the board. Mr. Boring put a mark next to it. "Please, continue. The floor's *all*" — his eyes roamed the room — "yours."

Cleo liked the sound of that. She swallowed and kept going. "My birth mom is the lady who gave birth to me" — she looked at Jimmy — "*obviously*. Before I was adopted." She had no problem with telling people she was adopted. It wasn't a big secret. "She named me Cleopatra because Cleopatra was a powerful and smart woman, and also a very beautiful African queen, and my birth mom wanted me to know that I'm these things too."

She held up her name tent and pointed to where she'd added her new middle name. "My middle name is Edison, which is my mom's unmarried name. My mom who adopted me, I mean. We are definitely related to the genius inventor and entrepreneur Thomas Edison, but don't ask me how, because I don't remember."

"But you're not really related if you're adopted, are you?" Jimmy blurted.

Mr. Boring eyed him, then added a second mark. "Did I mention that the three strikes program lasts all day long? There's a lot of day left, Jimmy."

"In *conclusion*" — Cleo pressed ahead with her prepared remarks, in spite of the warmth in her cheeks and the shakiness that had come over her — "my name is Cleopatra Edison Oliver, president of Cleopatra Enterprises, Inc.!" She ran her hand under her name tent with a flourish. "But you can just call me Cleo." She folded her hands on her desk and flashed them her best CEO smile. A few kids laughed, which was fine. She had meant for her audience to be entertained.

Jimmy raised his hand. Mr. Boring hesitated. "Yes, Jimmy?"

"Why did that woman want you to think you're a queen? You can't be a queen unless you're from a royal family."

Cleo scowled. Now she was getting mad.

"In her birth mom's eyes, I'm sure Cleo will always be a queen," Mr. Boring interjected.

A pain shot through her chest, as if her heart were a peeled orange and someone had stuck in their thumbs and pulled it into two sections.

Mr. Boring smiled at her. A nice smile.

Heat rushed to her face. Cleo blinked away the tears that had sprung to her eyes in a surprise attack.

"Thank you for sharing, Cleo. Micah?"

Cleo didn't hear anything of what Micah said. The Name Game had turned out to be The Lame Game. And a little bit The Shame Game. Anyway, it was a real stinker.

CHAPTER 6

On Top of the World
(For a Moment, Anyway)

After school, Cleo and Josh walked home. Normally, Caylee would join them, but that day, her mom picked her up for some kind of appointment.

In the kitchen, Mom was making something again. Bags of ingredients, messy bowls, measuring cups, and eggshells littered the counter. The Longevity Lollipops hadn't gone over so well. Cleo's had gotten stuck in her throat and practically choked her to death.

Mom turned off the mixer and gave them both kisses. "How was school?"

JayJay ran in and threw his arms around Cleo's waist. "Cleo!" It was nice to come home to an adoring fan. She hugged him back and he headed for Josh.

"Mom! Guess what?" Josh said. "Emilio's in my class!" He opened the pantry door, scavenging for a snack.

"That's great!"

"What are you making this time?" Cleo eyed the gritty batter suspiciously. It looked a little too much like something that had been digested once already.

"Quinoa Cupcakes!"

"Keen-what?"

Mom held up a bag of birdseed. "Keen-*wha*. It's a miracle grain. Full of protein. You can try one when they're done!"

"No thanks. I'll just have one of these." She grabbed a chocolate chip protein bar from the pantry and peeled back the wrapper. "Can I open my avocado stand today?"

"What about homework?"

"Our teacher doesn't believe in giving a lot of homework."

Mom eyed her skeptically. "Oh, really?"

"I've just got a little reading. I can do it in between customers."

"Okay, but you have to answer my question first. How was school?"

"Fine." Except for dumb Jimmy Ryerson asking her questions about her birth mom. She'd thought she'd gotten over it, but there it was again, making her feel weird, like she didn't belong. "I like Mr. Boring."

"He does seem like a good guy."

"You've met him?"

"I emailed your teachers last week. Just to introduce myself — and our family. Like I do every year." Of course. Cleo wished she wouldn't make such a big deal out of it, but Mom had made educating others about adoption one of her main missions in life.

"Well, I've got a business to run." Cleo started toward the family room, where she'd stashed all her business stuff. "You know where to find me."

Outside, the avocados on the ground were all half eaten. *Barkley.* He had ruined ten dollars' worth of product! The remaining avocados were high up in the branches. She got the ladder from their detached garage and set it up next to a tree.

She had just climbed to the top when their neighbor across the street, Ms. Chu, came outside in gardening gloves. Ms. Chu waved her little shovel in the air. "Cleo! That's too high! You're going to hurt yourself!"

"*Ni hao*, Ms. Chu!" This summer, Cleo had asked Ms. Chu to teach her Mandarin Chinese, the future language of businesspeople everywhere. "Want to *mai* some avocados today?" Cleo raised an avocado to show Ms. Chu. The ladder wobbled. Her heart did a double flip, but she kept her cool. CLEO'S AWESOME AVOCADOS was back in business!

"Just get down from there!" she said. "I'll get you the money. How much?"

"A dollar each!" Cleo had never done a business transaction from this far away. Or from a ladder. But so what? A sale was a sale!

"I pay the same at the store. What happened to the 'blowout sale'?" Ms. Chu never accepted full price.

"That was yesterday! But for you, I'll make it four for three dollars! Deal?"

"Deal! Now, you get down before you break your neck!"

Cleo was going to get down. Really she was.

And then she saw the roof.

And it was only a step away. A big step, but she knew she could do it. And if she *could* do it, then she had to do it. It was a law of the universe.

She plucked four avocados, then hurried down and dragged the ladder closer to the house, which was single-story in the front, double-story in the back, where they'd added on bedrooms.

She climbed to the top of the ladder again and pulled herself onto the roof, trying not to make noise. If Mom found her, she would have a cow. Not just a cow. A bull with horns. This was the kind of thing that would have her yelling Cleo's whole entire name to the whole entire neighborhood. *Cleopatra Lenore Oliver!!! Get down from there right now!*

But she didn't want to get down. She was a Capricorn, after all. Part mountain goat, according to

Fortune. Always climbing. Never satisfied until they reached the top. Cleo scrambled up the short slope to the pointy part in the middle.

She looked down on the roof of Miss Jean's chicken coop. Gloria, Alice, and Susan B pecked and scratched in the dirt yard. Big Betty was probably chilling out in the coop. Miss Jean had paid Cleo to chicken-sit a few times. Easy money. On the other side of Miss Jean's was the Williamses'. Cleo giggled at the underwear drying on a line in their backyard. It looked big enough to fit a giant panda.

Beyond the Williamses' single-story was Caylee's palace of a house. It was pink — which Caylee thought was horrific, but Cleo thought was splendarvelous — with red Spanish tiles on the roof and a side balcony just right for sipping their Tangy Tangerine Tonic™, which they'd made from the Ortegas' tangerine trees and sold earlier in the summer. The Ortegas' house stood out on their street like a flamingo in a flock of pigeons. It was exactly the kind of house Cleo would like to live in.

Caylee's bedroom window was open. Should she

yell? She might get caught, but on the other hand, if her best friend was home she would see her on top of her house.

She cupped her hands around her mouth. "Ca-a-a-y-l-e-e-e!" Caylee's gauzy blue curtains fluttered in her window. "Ca-a-a-y-l-e-e-e!"

Caylee didn't appear, but crouching there, on the pinnacle of the roof, Cleo suddenly felt on top of the world.

She put her feet on either side of the peak and stood straight up. *Wow-ee!* The view was amazing! She could see all the way to Audubon High School, where Dad taught computers and history. Dull, meaningless history. It was much more important to look ahead, to the future.

And she knew what the future held for her: more businesses. Because she was an entrepreneur. Just like Fortune. Probably like *lots* of people in her birth family.

An idea struck her so hard it practically knocked her from her perch.

She would start a business at school!!!

She could see it all now. Her desk would become her executive office, the nerve center of Cleopatra Enterprises, Inc. Caylee would be her COO — Chief Operating Officer — since she was the most organized person on the planet.

Just then, the sky exploded with noise and the whoosh of beating wings. A *hundred* wild parrots (she wasn't exaggerating, *really*, even though she had been known to, on occasion) landed in the camphor trees that towered over her house. They had been there before. They came and went around the neighborhood — a big, noisy, extended bird family. The fact that they had chosen to land right there, at the very moment she had this great thought . . . it was a sign! She just knew it was!

The birds squawked and flapped their wings as if they were cheering and clapping just for her.

Barkley ran outside, barking and jumping up on one of the giant trees. Josh ran after him. Cleo ducked.

"Mom! Mom! Cleo's on the roof!"

Corn dogs and Costco.

Ms. Chu came out on her front porch. She started waving and shouting too.

Between the parrots screeching, Barkley barking, Josh tattling, and Ms. Chu yelling, the corner of their street was louder than the floor of the New York Stock Exchange.

It was almost loud enough to drown out the sound of Mom yelling her whole entire name to the whole entire neighborhood.

CHAPTER 7

Power Lunch

Wednesday, Caylee was missing from school, which was a real bummer because Cleo was *dying* to tell her about the business she planned to start at New Heights — once she thought of one. Cleo had called her as soon as she could that afternoon, but Mrs. Ortega said Caylee wasn't feeling well and couldn't come to the phone.

Caylee was late to school on Thursday, but not too late to hear Mr. Boring make an incredible announcement: They would NOT be doing the usual fifth-grade Family Tree Project!

Cleo couldn't believe it. Mr. Boring had just become her favorite teacher ever.

"Raise your hands, please. What does it mean to have a *passion* for something?" He wrote the word *passion* on the board.

Cleo's hand shot into the air. Fortune was always talking about passion! It was Fortune Principle Number One: *Passion is purpose.*

"Cleo."

"A passion is something you *love* to do. It's how you know your purpose in life."

"Wow. Purpose in life. Yes. Great. Something that fires you up, that you like learning about or doing so much that you could learn about or do it all day long."

"Like robots?" Quentin asked. He'd been known around school as Computer-Head Quentin ever since he'd coded his own software in fourth grade.

"Sure! Robots could be a person's passion."

"My mom says hers is chocolate," Cole said.

"That could be a dangerous one, but yes, for

some people I suppose food is a passion." He looked around the room. "What about you? What's *your* passion?"

Cleo's mind was whirling.

"Nothing wrong with family trees, but I've got to make sure I don't live up to my *boring* name, so this year, in this class, we'll be doing *Passion Projects*."

Ooo . . . a Passion Project! Cleo loved the sound of that.

"This is your assignment . . ."

Ugh. There it was again. That word. Mr. Boring had gone the whole first two days of school without using it once. But she kept listening, because at least this time the assignment was connected to something that sounded splendarvelous!

In their projects, he went on to explain, they would prepare up-front presentations to give their classmates an experience of their passion.

She couldn't believe how *perfect* this was. Of course she would make the focus of her project the business that she planned to start at school! She straightened her name tent on her desk. Cleopatra Edison Oliver, CEO, was going to rock *this* assignment! All she needed now was a business idea.

Mr. Boring asked them to get out their journals and spend a few minutes listing their passions. After that, they would choose one and spend a few more minutes writing about that particular passion. They were "brainstorming," he said.

Cleo could brainstorm later. Right then, she needed to tell Caylee, her future COO, her plan.

She quietly ripped a page out of her journal and wrote:

Caylee,

Cleopatra Enterprises, Inc., is expanding into the school market!!! I need a new business idea. (Maybe your fantastic hair clips???) And a COO. Which of course needs to be you, since you are the most organized person in the whole entire world — and my BFF! Will you? Pretty please?? Here's to our future success!!!

XOXO, *Cleo*

P.S. I climbed onto the roof of our house the other day. It was awesome! I shouted your name, but I don't think you were home. Mom was mad, but thankfully she didn't ground me from TV, because Fortune was amazing (as usual). I've got to find a way to get on her show!!!

She folded the paper about sixteen times. On her way to sharpening her pencil, she quickly dropped the note into Caylee's lap. She watched from her place in line behind Computer-Head Quentin. Caylee read the note, then turned over the paper and scribbled a reply.

On Cleo's way back to her seat, they did another handoff. Fortunately, Mr. Boring was too busy asking

Micah to stop singing to notice. She slipped into her chair, waited for her teacher to go back to his writing, and read Caylee's response:

Of <u>course</u> I want to do it with you! I don't have any business ideas. How are you going to get on Fortune's show??!!

Your BFF, Caylee ☺

P.S. My clips take kind of a long time to make.

P.S.S. What's a COO???

She was so happy that Caylee Ortega was her friend. She found everything about her completely adorable, including the fact that she thought P.S.S. was the correct way to spell a second P.S. Cleo would convince Caylee about selling her clips, eventually. If she could make a paintbrush and palette, she could make anything. They would personalize them based on people's interests and hobbies! Done and done.

In the lunchroom, Cleo tried to avoid seeing Lexie Lewis but she was hard not to notice in her spangled, tiger-striped hoodie. As Cleo passed Lexie's class table, Lexie said something about a modeling shoot after school, in a super-loud voice.

Cleo barely noticed. Her mind was on more important matters: coming up with a new business.

She and Caylee sat across from Tessa and Steffy. Tessa greeted them with her big grin. "Steffy and I are doing gymnastics at recess. Want to come?"

"We can show you front handsprings," Steffy said. "We learned how this summer."

Cleo shook her head. "Thanks, but Caylee and I have an important meeting."

"We do?" Caylee's forehead wrinkled.

"For Cleopatra Enterprises, Inc."

"Oh. Okay." She shrugged. "I guess I'm busy."

"Maybe tomorrow?" Tessa bit on her bottom lip.

Tessa's big front teeth made Cleo think of a rabbit, which made her think of the carrots she wanted to trade. She scanned Tessa's lunch, spread out in front of her. And what a lunch it was! Mac and cheese. Mandarin oranges. A *pudding pack*.

Pudding! Cleo *loved* pudding. And it was chocolate, her favorite. But carrots, even with ranch dressing, wouldn't be enough to get a pudding. She'd have to throw in at least one sandwich cookie. She tried anyway.

"Hey, Tess, I'll trade you carrots and ranch dressing for your pudding."

Tessa shook her head. Cleo expected to hear, *No way!* Instead, Tessa said, "I can't eat carrots."

"You can't eat carrots?" Cleo wasn't a big carrot fan herself, but she had never heard of anyone having a carrot *allergy*.

"She means she can't eat carrots right *now*," Steffy said. "Her canine's loose."

"Huh?" Cleo was seriously confused. "Your dog ran away so you can't eat carrots?"

Everyone laughed. Even Caylee. Cleo chuckled a little, just so she wouldn't be the only one not laughing. "Not her dog, goofball," Steffy said. "Her *tooth*."

Cleo forced a little air out of her mouth — *puh!* — like, *Du-uh*. "I knew that. I was just making a joke." She forced a laugh, then got serious again. "Why don't you just use the other side?"

"They're loose on both sides," Tessa said. "I'm afraid of them coming out. It's going to hurt." No wonder her lunch foods were all so soft.

"I keep telling her they've got to come out eventually," Steffy said. "So why not just get it over with?"

"Seriously. That's what I've been telling my brother Josh."

"Plus, her Tooth Fairy pays a lot of money."

Cleo perked up. "How much?" she asked.

Tessa looked a little embarrassed. "Five dollars."

"A *tooth?*" Cleo shouted. Tessa nodded. Cleo made some quick calculations. "That means your mouth is worth one hundred bucks! More if you get your wisdom teeth out."

Cleo did a survey around the table. It was the same

for Steffy, Amelie, Quentin, Noah . . . even Caylee! Kids got *dollars*, not cents, for their teeth these days. Cole said he and Lexie got anywhere from five to ten dollars a tooth, depending on how generous the Tooth Fairy felt that day, or "whether she got a bonus in her paycheck that month."

At first, Cleo was miffed that all she got was a goofy poem about her latest lost tooth, two shiny new quarters, and a pack of sugar-free gum, but that didn't last for long because suddenly, as she looked out across the cafeteria, watching kids biting into their pizza and their celery sticks, she didn't see teeth. She saw a business opportunity.

Cleo crunched on a carrot. Yes, she had planned to trade, but she'd just been given some incredible information. This was big. Way bigger than carrot sticks. It wouldn't make her a multimillionaire, but a ready-made audience sat all around her.

She had gotten her next business idea!

At recess, Cleo and Caylee ran to their spot on the grassy hillside. "I now call to order the first official executive meeting of Cleopatra Enterprises, Inc.!" Cleo opened her notebook.

"Agenda Item Number One." She planned to launch right into her business proposal, but Caylee was staring out at the field, not paying attention at all. "Earth to Jelly — come in, Jelly."

"Oh, sorry. Did you say something?"

"Not really. Not yet. Just starting our meeting." She paused. She was dying to get to her latest business idea. "Why weren't you at school yesterday? I tried to call you. Is something wrong?"

Caylee shrugged. She picked at the grass around her shoes. "Just my dad . . ."

Of course. What a dumb question. A *lot* was wrong in Caylee's world. Mr. Ortega had left his family four months ago. *How could a parent just walk out like that?* "He could come back." She didn't sound very convincing, even to herself.

Caylee picked a clover and flopped onto her back.

"He opened a new car lot in Palm Springs. He bought another house." She rolled onto her side. "He has a *girlfriend.*"

It was true. It didn't look good. Cleo thought of Nana's pet name for Pops. "What a *nincompoop.*"

Caylee giggled. Cleo laughed too. She always laughed at that word. She said it over and over, sliding her voice up and down, stretching out one syllable and then another — "Your dad is a niiiiiiiin-compoop! Nin-com-POOOOOP!" — until her stomach ached from laughing and Caylee was spread-eagle on the grass and wiping tears from her eyes.

Caylee let out a big breath. "So, what are we meeting about, anyway?"

"I've got an idea for a new business — something we can do while I wait for you to make a bunch of barrettes." She grinned. "*Teeth!*"

Caylee's eyebrows pulled together. "Huh?"

"A tooth-pulling business! Tessa — and lots of others, even you — you all get plenty of money for your baby teeth, right?"

"Ri-i-i-ght . . ."

"So, we're going to pull out loose teeth for a small percentage of people's Tooth Fairy money!"

Caylee thought for a moment. "But why would people pay *you* when they can do it themselves? Or maybe go to a *dentist?*"

"Dentists are expensive. And you heard Tessa. She's afraid of it hurting." Cleo looked out onto the field where Tessa was doing a backhand walkover. Steffy was trying to help Mia Jeffers, but Mia was stuck in the backbend part. Lexie Lewis stood nearby, shouting, "Just flip your legs over!" As if she were the expert. Cleo would like to see *her* try.

Caylee still looked skeptical. "So you're going to find a way to pull teeth without it hurting?"

"Possibly . . . How do *you* do it?"

"What?"

"Pull out your loose teeth?"

Caylee's eyes looked one way and her mouth scrunched to the other. "I guess I just wait a super-long time until they're really loose, and then it doesn't hurt so bad. But it still hurts. It always hurts."

Cleo thought about her own teeth that had come

out. "Okay, maybe you're right. But I still think we can make it work. So, are you with me?"

"I don't know . . ."

"Come on, Cay-Cay!" Cleo shook Caylee's arm. "You've got to believe in yourself!"

Caylee squinted. Her squished face made it look as if she had just tasted something rotten.

Cleo jumped to her feet, pulling Caylee up with her. "As Fortune Principle Number Three says" — she punched her fist in the air — " 'Doubt is more deadly than failure!' "

CHAPTER 8

Brainstorming

Before parting ways in front of Cleo's house, Cleo charged Caylee with the task of thinking up quick and painless ways to pull teeth.

"It won't be painless. It's *never* painless," Caylee reminded her.

"Right. Quick, then. The quicker the better. And creative. Kids might want to try it just for the experience if we make it crazy enough."

"Crazy is *your* department. But I'll try. See you tomorrow." Caylee hitched her backpack onto her shoulders and walked toward her house.

Inside, Cleo headed straight for her room. She had to go through the kitchen.

Mom was running the mixer again, stirring up some more batter. Tuesday's creation, the Quinoa Cupcakes, had tasted *disgusting*. Cleo had told her it'd be false advertising to call them cupcakes, which were, by definition, delicious.

"Hello to you too!" Mom called, but Cleo was already halfway up the stairs. Barkley barked from below. Poor dog, he'd gotten so fat he didn't even want to *try* climbing. She came back down and kissed the top of his head. "Sorry, Barks. I need to focus right now."

"Everything okay?" Mom asked.

"Fantastic, actually. Mr. Boring isn't making us do that dumb family tree project!"

Mom looked surprised. "Really? Wow. Okay. I guess you're glad, huh?"

"Yes, I'm glad. How was *I* supposed to do a family tree?"

Mom's eyelids fluttered. Her voice stutter-stepped before continuing. "Well, we talked about that, remember? We decided you would put me and your dad, and Nana and Pops, and Gran and Grandpa Edison, and your brothers —"

"I know, I know. But, Mom, listen, instead of the family tree, we get to do *Passion Projects*! Just like Fortune: 'Passion is purpose!' I can't wait! I'm going to focus on starting a business. And I already have my next idea!"

"Which is?" Mom tasted her batter. "Mmm . . . not bad."

"Can I tell you later? Please? I need to brainstorm — and write a paragraph describing my project. It's our homework." That was the magic word with Mom.

"Don't let *me* stop you."

Cleo clambered back upstairs and closed the door behind her. Time to get to work.

She faced her brainstorming easel. Mr. Boring had taught them a creative-thinking technique called *webbing* and this was the perfect opportunity to use it. She wrote the words *loose teeth* in red pen on the white board and circled them. Whatever the word (or words) in the circle made you think, you wrote it down. Then you circled the new word and connected it with a line to the word that made you think it. Doing this helped dislodge ideas that were stuck in your brain. *Free associating*, Mr. Boring had called it.

She wrote *pull* in a bubble and connected it to *loose teeth*. That made her think of taffy, which she'd seen being pulled and stretched on a machine in a candy store once. Maybe she could sell kids taffy and they would bite into it, and *voilà!* — their teeth would come out in the taffy! It had potential. But it wasn't surefire.

What tool would basically guarantee success each and every time? She wrote *tool* on her board and connected it to *pull*.

Pliers?

Too scary.

Hammer?

Too violent.

She was critiquing. She wasn't supposed to be critiquing. Mr. Boring had told them to spend at least ten minutes free associating and to save the critiquing for later.

Downstairs, Josh started screaming. Julian was wailing. Mom was shouting. How was she supposed to come up with an inspired idea with all this racket? Her brainstorm was quickly becoming a brain drizzle.

Teeth. Teeth. How had she gotten hers out? By twisting, she realized. She drew another line from *loose teeth* and wrote *twist* in a bubble. That made her think of *twirl,* which made her think of Mom's beaters twirling around and around.

Wait a minute . . . what if she connected a loose tooth to an electric mixer with a piece of string and turned the mixer on? That tooth would go *flying* out of the person's mouth! She wrote *mixer* and connected it to *twirl.* Now she was getting somewhere!

"Cleo!" Mom's voice interrupted her moment of inspiration. "Cleo!!"

She opened her door. "What?" she shouted back.

"Come down here, please!"

"I'm still doing my homework!"

"Just come down here. Now!"

Cleo huffed and plodded downstairs. Josh was nowhere in sight. Jay's arms were draped over Mom's shoulders and his face was buried in her neck. "Would you keep them entertained for a little bit? Please, sweetie? You're so good at it."

This was the not-so-great thing about having lots of great ideas — or little brothers, for that matter. She got called on, often, to keep Josh and Jay out of trouble. "But I'm working!"

"I just need to get these in the oven. Half hour, at the most."

"Why are you doing all this baking, anyway?" Cleo asked.

"Actually, I'm trying to come up with something original to sell —"

"*Sell?* Where? I could help you!"

"At the farmer's market, and I'm sure you could. But first I need your help with the boys. So . . . could you?" She set Julian down. He ran to the family room.

"Oh-*kay*."

Mom kissed her forehead. "Thank you. I'll get Josh out of time-out."

Cleo found JayJay standing over the wreckage of what likely had been a LEGO building. His shoe-string arms were tied across his chest, his fists little knots at the ends. "Josh messed up my fort."

Pieces and soldiers lay scattered everywhere. "Yeah. I can see that."

Mom came back. "Josh is going to read. You two go on."

Cleo scooped up a handful of soldiers, suddenly energized. "Come on, JayJay. I've got an idea!"

They lined up plastic soldiers on the boys' bedroom windowsill and took turns shooting them down with Josh's Nerf gun missiles. Then they made parachutes by taping dental floss to Kleenexes, tied the soldiers to the missiles, and shot the soldiers from the top bunk like paratroopers, except that they more just dive-bombed to the floor because the Kleenexes weren't strong enough. Or the missiles were too heavy.

Cleo didn't know, and she didn't really care. Science wasn't her thing.

As she launched another paratrooper, a phrase appeared on the white board of her mind. *Nerf gun.* Of course. It was the *perfect* tool for tooth pulling! And she wouldn't need to convince Mom to let her borrow the mixer, which would be impossible, anyway.

She had found the answer. She would *shoot* people's teeth out. All she needed was to test her method, and the perfect guinea pig was right downstairs, reading a book.

CHAPTER 9

Paratrooper Tooth

"Josh! Josh! You've got to see this!" Cleo bounded into the living room. JayJay slid on the wood floor and crashed into her.

Josh didn't take his eyes off his book. "What?"

"You'll see." She grabbed his arm. "Let's just say it involves your Nerf gun and flying teeth."

Josh's head snapped up. "You never asked if you could use my Nerf gun."

"May I use your Nerf gun? Come on, you'll think this is so cool!"

Josh shut his book and stomped behind them through the kitchen.

"Everything all right?" Mom asked, pulling a pan of lumpy cookies from the oven. Cookies that looked like they could choke a yak.

"Great!" Cleo said, zipping past before Mom could ask if she wanted to try one. Did Mom realize customers liked lollipops, cupcakes, and cookies to taste *good*?

"You sure?" Mom's eyes had a *What are you up to now?* look in them. Cleo leaped up the stairs before she could ask more questions.

"Sure!"

As soon as they got to the boys' room, Cleo hit Josh with her sales pitch. She kept her voice low. "You want your loose tooth out, right?"

He squinted one eye and looked at her warily — like a fish eyeing a shark. "I don't know. Why?"

"What if I told you you could have it out today? That you could get your quarters and gum this very night."

His lips pooched out, and the space between his eyebrows got all wrinkly. He thought she was trying to pull a fast one.

"I'm not trying to trick you, Josh. I'm letting you be my first customer! I'll even make this first time on the house."

"You're not supposed to go on the house any-more." Julian looked up from his plastic-soldier battle. "Mom said."

"'On the house' means for free, JayJay. I'm going to let Josh be my first customer for *free*." She grinned.

"What do you mean 'customer'?" Josh said. "What's that got to do with my tooth?"

"What's a customer?" Julian asked.

Oh, man. JayJay had so much to learn. "A cus-tomer is someone who buys a product or a service from someone else — like the people who bought our avocados." She spoke to Josh again. "In this case, you would be buying the service of me taking out your tooth. Except I'm not going to charge you — this time."

Josh's eyes got huge. "*You?* Unh-unh. No way."

"*Please*, Josh. It'll be so fast you probably won't even feel it."

He narrowed his eyes. "You'll probably make it hurt on purpose."

That stung, but she brushed it off. She had a business transaction to complete. "Actually . . . I won't be doing it. Your Nerf gun will."

Josh's forehead bunched again, and his lips were all stitched up. "What do you mean?"

Cleo held up the floss she'd nabbed from the bathroom. "I'll take a piece of this, tie one end around the Nerf missile and the other end around your loose tooth. Then I pull the trigger, and — *shazam!* — your tooth is soaring through the air."

"Like a paratrooper?" he said slowly.

"*Just* like a paratrooper," Cleo said.

A smile spread across his face.

She got another flash of inspiration. "I'll be right back. Don't try to do it while I'm gone!" She rushed out of the room.

Mom talked on the phone downstairs. "I wonder

if we could work out a deal, Jean. I need cage-free eggs for my products. You have cage-free chickens."

Miss Jean. Perfect. Mom would be on the phone for a while. Miss Jean liked to talk.

Cleo headed to the room at the end of the hall to find Dad's new tablet. Getting sent to her room for taking Mom's knife tickled the edges of her memory, but she swept the thought aside and kept on going.

She found the tablet in its drawer. She stared at it. Should she? Her parents had made it absolutely clear that she was not to use it without permission. If only she'd realized the can of Pepsi had tipped over on the last one. Unfortunately, she'd been horsing around with JayJay and left the tablet marinating in soda.

She *needed* to record this momentous event. The opportunity to capture her tooth-pulling method on video might not come again for weeks or even months. And she would be careful. *Super-duper careful.* No electronic devices would be harmed in the making of *this* film! She grabbed it and ran back to the boys' room, closing the door behind her.

Julian was dropping plastic soldiers off the top bunk, making explosion sounds when they hit the ground. Barkley — *Yay, Barkley! He'd actually made it up the stairs* — stood below, trying to catch them in midair. He snatched one in his mouth, lay down, and went to town on it.

"No, Barkley!" Josh yanked the soldier from Barkley's stinky mouth and wiped the slobbery toy on his pants. "What are you doing with that?" He watched Cleo turn on the tablet. "Aren't you supposed to —"

"I'm going to record your paratrooper tooth!"

His eyes lit up. "Cool! Then I'll be able to watch it."

You and a whole lot of other people, Cleo thought. Her marketing plan was taking shape even as she loaded her tooth-pulling instrument.

Her extractor.

No. Her *Extractor Extraordinaire!*™

She tied a long piece of floss to the missile. Julian climbed down the ladder. "You gonna hurt Joshy?"

She took the loose end of the floss. "No. I'm helping him. Aren't I, Josh?" She smiled, thinking about all the dangly toothed kids at New Heights Elementary.

Josh suddenly looked unsure. Time to take charge. It was Fortune Principle Number Four: *Confidence inspires confidence.* And right then, Cleo's young followers needed to believe that she knew what she was doing, even if she wasn't one hundred percent sure herself.

"It's going to be great. Think of the story that you can tell at school. And you won't have to go to sleep terrified you're going to swallow your tooth again."

Josh nodded, but his eyebrows were still pulled together.

Cleo forged ahead. She made a slipknot at the end of the floss, put it around Josh's tooth, and cinched it tight.

"Is it going to hurt? It's going to hurt." Josh shook his head. "I don't want to! I changed my mind!" He'd been a chicken about the other teeth too.

She handed him the Extractor. "Here. You can even pull the trigger." She put the tablet in camera mode and held it up.

"But —" Josh protested.

"I want to take a picture!" Julian shouted. Barkley started barking. JayJay jumped onto her arm, jostling the tablet. Cleo sucked in her breath as it slipped through her hands. She bobbled it a couple times but grabbed it before it hit the ground.

"Dummy, you almost made me drop it!"

JayJay's bottom lip started to do its Jell-O Jigglers thing. His big brown eyes watered.

Barkley was still barking. "Quiet, Barks!" She didn't need Mom coming to investigate. "I'm sorry, JayJay. I shouldn't have called you that. You can take a picture after me. Promise." She put her arm around him, feeling bad for making him cry. "I just need you to watch for now, okay?"

"Okay." He sat on his bed. Barkley sat on the floor with his chin on JayJay's knee.

One brother down. One to go.

"Do this, Josh, and you'll be able to tell Emilio. He'll think it's super cool. I bet all the boys will think it's cool."

He looked from the Nerf gun to the tablet and back to the Nerf gun. "Okay . . . I'll try it."

Bingo!

She pushed the RECORD button. "Say hello to Joshua Myron Oliver, client of Cleo's Quick and Painless Tooth Removal Service." Josh stood there, staring like a dummy. "Wave to the viewers, please."

Josh raised his hand, but his smile looked pasted on. Better than nothing.

Cleo turned the camera on herself. "Here at Cleo's Quick and Painless Tooth Removal Service" — an important rule of any advertisement was that it should repeat the name of the company at least three times — "we let the customer be in control." She put the camera back on Josh. "Whenever you're ready, Mr. Oliver, just pull the trigger."

Barkley started barking again.

"*Barkley!* Quiet!"

Josh shook his head. He was wimping out. "I dohn wah doo," he said with his mouth open. Drool spilled over his lip.

Great. Nothing like a little drool to win over the customers.

"Of course, we understand at *Cleo's Quick and*

Painless Tooth Removal Service that not everyone is excited to say good-bye to their teeth —" Cleo lunged for the Nerf gun.

She wasn't sure who actually pulled the trigger. The missile rocketed toward the window. Josh screamed bloody murder and clutched his mouth. JayJay jumped up and down, shrieking. Barkley barked like mad.

Cleo ran to pick up the missile and held it out in front of the tablet. Dangling from the end of the floss was one beautiful baby tooth. *Ka-ching!*

Josh rushed for his tooth. "Give that to me. That's worth money!"

She handed it to him, still attached to the missile. "Smile for the camera!"

He smiled for real this time, showing off a nice big gap where his top front tooth had been. "It worked!" he shouted.

She zoomed in on his mouth. "So, folks, as you can see, this is one satisfied customer!"

The doorknob turned. *Mom!* Cleo slung the tablet

along the floor. It zipped across the carpet and disappeared under the bunk bed.

"What in the world?" Mom said, stepping into the room. "What's going on in here?"

"My tooth came out! My tooth came out! We did it with my Nerf gun!" Josh held up the missile. The tooth swung on the floss.

"Your Nerf gun?" Mom's jaw dropped.

"We even got it on —"

"On the first try!" Cleo said before Josh could finish, just in case he'd been about to say they'd recorded it — on the tablet she didn't have permission to use.

"Yeah! Isn't that so cool, Mom?" He ran to Cleo and threw his arms around her. "Thanks, Cleo!"

Her heart suddenly felt all soft like room-temperature butter. "You're welcome." She squeezed back.

Mom put her hand on Josh's head. "I guess Mr. Tooth Fairy will be making a visit to our house tonight." He nodded excitedly.

"It's my turn to take a picture!" JayJay tugged on Cleo's arm.

Mom looked at JayJay, then at Cleo. The questioning look was back on her face.

"Uh . . . I told him he could use my camera."

Julian kept tugging. "But —"

"Come on, JayJay. Let's go get it." She took his hand. She needed to get him out of here pronto, before he spilled the beans.

Mom asked to see the tooth. She held the missile, laughing. "Cleo, how *do* you come up with this stuff?"

Cleo smiled. What could she say? She was inspired. With a little luck and some word-of-Josh's-mouth advertising, she would be turning a profit in no time.

CHAPTER 10

Drumming Up Business

The next morning, Cleo was up and ready to go a half hour early. She'd gone to Caylee's right after *Fortune* with Dad's tablet stashed in her backpack and asked Caylee's older brother, Ernie Junior, to upload the video of Josh onto YouTube. He'd gone above and beyond, even adding a slow-motion replay of the tooth shooting from Josh's mouth. It was awesome. And hilarious. *Hilarisome.* Hopefully, Mom and Dad would agree . . . once she told them about it.

Now the tablet was safely back in its drawer, Josh was parading around the house with his sugar-free gum and fifty cents, and Cleo had a stack of advertisements in her backpack, ready to hand out at school. Cleo pulled out a copy of the ad and read it over one more time.

CLEO'S QUICK AND (nearly) PAINLESS* TOOTH REMOVAL SERVICE

We pull them out so you don't have to!!!

Got a wiggler? Loose tooth getting you down? **WORRY NO MORE!** With our *highly effective* method, we'll have you back enjoying Twizzlers and tortilla chips before you can say "Tooth Fairy."
Watch it work at: <u>www.youtube.com/watch?v=8iQjy0ZuMs</u>

*You're not going to **believe** your eyes!!!*
Your parents will be thanking us!

Get your teeth pulled as quickly as **"Ready, aim, FIRE!"**

WHERE: WILSON PARK PLAYGROUND
WHEN: THIS Saturday between 10 and 2
COST: Only $1 per tooth

For **just $2** more we'll record your extraction so you can watch your tooth fly over and over again!!! *(Recordings are great for sharing with grandparents.)* **20% of profits to go to Horizon Home**** for homeless moms and their kids.

*Method is guaranteed to be quick. Pain may vary.
**A Tooth Fairy–approved charity

Caylee had suggested that they add the "nearly" before "PAINLESS." She'd also talked Cleo out of trying to operate this particular business on school grounds. All guns, including toy ones, were completely off-limits and could even get a kid suspended. It had happened to Ronnie Tipton just last year.

Cleo still thought Caylee needed to take more risks, but this time she knew Caylee was right. They would offer their service at Wilson Park, not far from the school.

Cleo lay on her bed, talking to Fortune about her latest venture. "I'm giving away twenty percent this time — because of what I saw on your show yesterday, about socially conscious being the new business model." She would show how *un*selfish she could be.

Fortune's eyes stayed put, her arms still frozen in that almost-hug.

"Because running businesses isn't only about making money. It's about making the world better for people, right?"

Cleo was sure Fortune's sparkly eyes were saying, "Absolutely! Girl, you've got it!"

Had she received Cleo's letter yet? Cleo realized with a start that it had been four days! The thought filled her with hope. Fortune might be holding Cleo's stationery at that very moment.

Cleo stood on the bed. She pressed her palms against Fortune's outstretched hands. Looked deep into her Magic 8 Ball eyes. And wished she could be Fortune's daughter.

Cleo had the flyers out of her backpack long before she, Caylee, and Josh reached school. She gave them to kids they passed on the way. She pressed them into kids' hands at the crosswalk. She gave some to Josh to give to his friends. As soon as they hit the playground, she handed Caylee a bunch too. "Let's split up. We'll get more done that way."

Caylee hesitated. "But you're better at talking to people about these things — I mean, talking people *into* things."

What could she say? It was her superpower, persuasion — or as she thought of it, Persuasion Power™, a set of skills that she planned to package and market as a series of business-success seminars with titles such as, "Stop Whining, Start Winning" and "Charm Them to Disarm Them: How to Be So Cute They Can't Say No."

"Okay, we'll stick together. For now. At first recess we'll split up."

Caylee looked relieved.

Cleo spotted Tessa playing tetherball with Steffy. With two loose teeth, Tessa was a top prospect. Unfortunately, Lexie Lewis waited to take on the winner.

So what, Cleo thought. She wouldn't let Lexie Lewis get in the way of making a sale. In fact, she might even have a loose tooth in that big mouth of hers. Cleo would get Lexie Lewis to use her business! The thrill of conquest drove her to the tetherball pole. Caylee trailed along.

Steffy had just beaten Tessa, who stepped out of the circle so Lexie could have her turn.

"Oh good, LeSnore is here. I can beat her next."
Lexie's lips curled into a power-hungry smile.

"In case you hadn't heard, my middle name is
Edison."

"Edison! That's a *boy's* name." Lexie Lewis
cackled.

Cleo ignored the jab. "Yes. I am now Cleopatra
Edison Oliver, CEO and president of Cleopatra Enterprises, Inc."

"That's not even a real company." Lexie smirked
and folded her arms.

"Come on, Lexie. Let's play," Steffy urged.

"*Corporation*, actually. I'm here to tell you about
my latest business." She handed flyers to Tessa,
Steffy, Lexie, and the few other girls waiting for a turn
to play.

"Tooth removal?" Lexie looked aghast. "Why
would I ever let *you* touch my teeth?"

Cleo was ready. Her superpower surged. "Well,
since you asked . . . You know that awful feeling of
having a loose tooth, and how you don't want *anything*

to touch it because every time it wiggles it makes you think of pain and blood?"

Lexie Lewis was actually listening. Cleo saw begrudging agreement in the girl's light brown eyes.

"Ooo, yeah, and that gross squishy stuff that's in the hole that's left behind!" Tessa said. "It feels like something you'd find in a tide pool — all furry and yucky."

They were getting off track. Cleo wanted them to *want* their teeth out, not fear the holes left behind. "And you spend weeks worrying about how you're going to get your tooth out and when will you be able to eat crunchy things again and what if you accidentally swallow it in your sleep?"

Tessa's normally big eyes got even bigger. "That happens?"

"Oh, yeah. My little brother swallowed his."

"Eww," Lexie said, dropping the flyer and grabbing the ball. "That means he pooped it out!" Mia, Steffy, and Taylor laughed. "Were you the one who found it?" They laughed again. Lexie hurled the ball.

The chain clanged as she and Steffy swatted it back and forth.

Cleo focused on Tessa. "Look, those teeth need to come out. Am I right?"

Tessa's mouth twitched as she tested one of the loose canines with her tongue.

"And you must *really* miss eating Tootsie Rolls." Cleo was glad she remembered her friend's favorite candy.

"Yeah, I do."

"I can *help* you, Tess! It will be easy and quick — so quick you'll barely feel it." She pointed to the flyer. "Watch this video on YouTube. Then come to Wilson Park tomorrow morning. I'll have it done for you in no time."

"I'll record it for you too if you want," Caylee added.

"And we're giving away *twenty* percent of what we make to a really good cause," Cleo said.

Steffy came over. She had lost the game to Lexie, who was now pounding Mia.

Time to close this deal. "So, will you come?"

"Umm . . . I don't know. Maybe." Tessa read the ad again.

"I'll go with you," Steffy said.

The recess monitor blew her whistle. Kids swarmed like bees, headed for their lines. Cleo stayed put, waiting for Tessa's answer.

Mia and Taylor had started toward their classroom, but Lexie had to butt in one last time. "You're crazier than I thought if you let *this* girl pull your teeth."

Tessa grinned. She *looked* a little crazy. "I'll be there!" she said.

Cleo let out a little whoop of glee and wrapped her arms around Tessa. "Thanks, Tessa! I knew you'd do it!"

Lexie Lewis rolled her eyes and walked away.

But Cleopatra *Edison* Oliver didn't care. She had won her first customer!

In class, Mr. Boring started off by asking for volunteers to read their Passion Project paragraphs. Cleo raised her hand right away, but he called on several other kids first. Quentin would be doing his on robot building — no surprise there. Amelie planned to conduct a songwriting workshop. Cool! Cleo had never tried to write a song. Maybe she could even come up with a jingle for her tooth-pulling business.

Noah's passion was race cars. Steffy's was gymnastics, and Tessa's, horse rescue. Cole was still deciding between taiko — a kind of Japanese drum — and trading cards. Mr. Boring enthusiastically recommended the cards. Ms. Sanchez, the teacher next door, might not appreciate drums.

The big surprise was Rowdy Jimmy Ryerson. His passion was gardening — with his grandpa.

"Gardening?" Cole blurted, interrupting Jimmy's paragraph. Cleo had been thinking the same thing. Good thing she hadn't said it out loud. Cole got a strike for that.

Caylee never raised her hand. Cleo hadn't thought

to ask what her best friend planned to do. Every time they'd gotten together lately, they'd talked about Cleo's project.

Finally, Mr. Boring called on Cleo. "My passion," she began reading, "is *business*. Starting *new* businesses is especially thrilling to me. I made my first sale when I was two years old. It was a Disney princess sticker to a man who didn't speak English. He gave me a whole dollar for it! Since then, I have sold many things. One day, I plan to run a huge corporation. My latest venture is a tooth-pulling business" — she held up a flyer — "Cleo's Quick and Painless" — she left out the *nearly* this time (people could read the fine print themselves) — "Tooth Removal Service. In my Passion Project presentation, I will talk about my business and how well it is going." She looked up from her paper and grinned.

"I see we have an *entrepreneur* in our midst." Mr. Boring wrote the word *entrepreneur* on the board. Under that, he wrote *enterprising*. "Cleo, I love your" — he pointed to the board — "*enterprising* spirit. Thank you for giving us two more vocabulary words for next week's spelling test." A few kids groaned, but not Cleo. She could spell those words in her sleep.

"May I pass out copies of my ad?"

"Sure!"

She started with Mr. Boring, then continued around the room.

Mr. Boring chuckled. "Before you can say 'Tooth Fairy,' eh? And what exactly is your 'quick and *nearly* painless' method?"

"I use my Extractor Extraordinaire (trademark)!"

"Love it!" He laughed again, then raised an eyebrow. "What *is* your Extractor Extraordinaire (trademark), and is it safe?"

"You'll have to come to the park to find out — or watch this video online." She pointed to the YouTube link. "And yes, it's safe. Absolutely. I tested it on my brother. It's all in the video."

"Intriguing."

Cleo buzzed with excitement. "I know you can pull your own teeth for free," she said to the class, "but when you use my service, you're also helping homeless moms and their kids." She pointed to the ad where it said she was giving away twenty percent of her profits to Horizon Home.

"So, this is sort of a fund-raiser as well as a business," Mr. Boring said.

"It's a *socially conscious* business," she said. For a flash, she felt like Fortune.

"This is great, Cleo. I'm really impressed," Mr. Boring said.

He was so impressed that during lunch he copied more flyers for her and asked some of the other teachers if she could advertise her business in their classes as well.

Cleo couldn't believe it. By the end of the day, almost everyone at New Heights Elementary knew about Cleo's Quick and Painless Tooth Removal Service. The only people left to tell were her parents.

CHAPTER 11

Risk Management

O n their walk home, Cleo told Caylee about going from class to class that afternoon, promoting her business. "Lexie Lewis looked like she was going to vomit the whole time I was talking."

"Was she sick?" Josh lagged behind, banging his lunch box against every street sign and lamppost.

Cleo threw her hands up in the air. "Why won't she just leave me alone already?"

Caylee looked sympathetic, but she had nothing to say.

"If only I hadn't been chosen to be her Welcome Ambassador when she came to New Heights last year."

"Yeah, I don't think she's liked you much since that first day when you accidentally knocked a tray of spaghetti into her lap."

Cleo grimaced. "She was wearing brand-new white jeans. Who wears white jeans?" Lexie Lewis, that was who.

"I think she's just jealous that people like you and they don't really like *her*."

Cleo thought about that. Could Lexie Lewis actually be jealous of her? It seemed impossible, but Caylee made a good point. *Was* there anything to like about Lexie?

They reached Cleo's house. "See you tomorrow. You'll have your camera, right?" Caylee had agreed to bring the super-nice camera her dad had bought her on her last visit. It could record videos as well as take pictures.

"Sure. See you tomorrow." Caylee kept walking.

Cleo turned to her brother. "I need to borrow your Nerf gun."

"Why?"

"For my business, of course."

"What are you going to give me?"

She crossed her arms. "Give you? I *gave* you the Nerf gun!"

"Only part of it." His lips pursed. He made a clicking sound with his tongue against his teeth. "I'll rent it to you for a dollar."

"*Rent?*" When had her brother become such a business shark?

An idea sprang into her mind. "I know! I'll let you be in a picture with everyone who gets a tooth out. Since you're the star of the video." That might be worth something, she thought, getting to take a picture with the kid on YouTube.

He smiled. "Am I going to be famous?"

She wrapped her arm around his neck, grateful he'd moved on from the rental thing. "Stick with me, kid, and you just might be."

She rolled out her business over dinner, telling her parents all about going around the school to promote it, and how she would use the same method she had on Josh, and her plans to give twenty percent of the profits to Horizon Home. The only thing she left out was the one tiny detail of her and Josh being on YouTube — and the fact that she'd used the tablet without permission to film themselves.

She couldn't tell them. Not yet. Mom might shut down her business again, and Cleo couldn't risk that. Practically the whole school knew about it. She could have dozens of customers!

Mom took a deep breath. "Cleo, I can tell you're excited about this, but did it ever cross your mind to check with us first — before going out and telling the whole world?"

"I'm checking with you now."

"No you're not. You're telling us what you've already done!" Mom looked exasperated.

Two green beans hung from Josh's lips, like fangs. Julian stuck one up his nose. Josh laughed, spewing his beans and little pieces of green muck onto the table. "Boys!" Mom was mad. Cleo had been laughing too. She bit her lip to stop.

"Your mom's right, Cleo," Dad said. "It's always better to get us on board first."

Okay. So she had mixed up the order of things a bit. Time for Persuasion Power™! "It's for school, Mom. I *need* to do it — for my Passion Project!"

"I'm not saying you can't do it —"

Cleo squealed. "Thank you!"

"Hold on."

Uh-oh. What was the catch?

"Maybe we should have people sign a liability release form."

"A what?"

"A form that says people can't sue us. Standard risk management." Before the boys, Mom had worked at Saint Luke's Hospital, making sure the hospital wouldn't get sued.

"Mom, sometimes you just have to take a risk and not worry so much about it."

Dad raised an eyebrow. A smile crinkled the corners of his mouth.

"Whatever you're thinking, you can keep it to yourself," Mom warned.

"No one's going to sue us, Mom. It works! You saw it! Right, Joshy?"

"Right!"

Mom looked at Josh, a smile on her lips at last. "Okay."

"Yay!" Cleo jumped up and squeezed her mom. "Thankyouthankyouthankyou!" Mom's head bobbled as Cleo jiggled up and down.

"But we're *all* going with you."

Cleo didn't protest. Mom had said yes!

"I have a soccer game, remember?" Dad said.

"Oh . . . right. Well, the boys and I will go, then."

Cleo could barely contain her excitement. She jiggled Mom some more. "Thank you!"

Mom narrowed her eyes and bit her lip, as if she were thinking. She wasn't changing her mind, was she? "I have an idea." She went to the kitchen and brought back a big baggie full of the lumpy cookies from the day before. They looked like something from the Natural History Museum — like plasticized armadillo poo. "What would you think about doing a little test marketing for me? You can hand them out to your customers."

Cleo eyed the cookies. "Are they any good?"

"That's what I want to find out!" Mom sat again. "Since you think I need to take more risks." She held out the bag. "Want to try one?"

"That's a risk I'm not sure I'm ready for," Cleo said.

Dad stifled a laugh.

Mom shook the bag. "Come on. They're breakfast cookies!"

"Cookies for breakfast?" Mom was working some persuasion power of her own. "Now, *that's* a great idea!" Cleo nodded in approval. "But they still have to taste good."

Barkley barked from his spot under the table. He didn't bother standing up. "Sorry, Barkley, not for you," Mom said, and pulled out a cookie.

Josh grabbed it.

"Me too!" JayJay shouted.

"Ew!" Josh's nose wrinkled. "They stink!" He dropped the cookie back in the bag.

"As I was saying . . ." Cleo crossed her arms.

"Josh!" Mom fished it out again. "You can't touch it and put it back in."

Mom tipped the bag toward Dad. He raised a hand and shook his head. "I'm pretty full from dinner, thanks."

Cleo sniffed the cookies. They smelled like something familiar . . . black licorice, maybe? "What's in them?" she asked.

Mom ticked off the ingredients on her fingers. "Let's see . . . amaranth flour, oats, organic cage-free eggs, prune juice —"

"Prune juice?" Josh stuck out his tongue. "Yuck!" He and Jay ran from the room. Dad started clearing the table.

Mom continued listing ingredients. "Dried apples, cinnamon, anise . . ."

"What's that?"

"A seed that tastes like licorice."

"And smells like it too," Cleo said. She pinched her nose.

"Anise is good for your digestion and your breath. A great way to start your day!"

"That could be your slogan!" Cleo said, still excited about Mom's business venture, even if the cookies didn't sound — or smell — very appetizing. "I'll try one tomorrow," Cleo said. Her stomach was feeling a little shaky, although she wasn't about to mention that to Mom. She didn't want Mom to have any reason to keep her home on her business's launch day.

Mom shrugged. "Suit yourself." She zipped up the baggie. "I'll need your help with a name for them — you're good at that — and let's keep working on a slogan."

Cleo tapped her cheek. She and her mom had never brainstormed for a business together. This would be fun! "Hmmm . . . how about, 'Nicki's Breakfast Cookies: *They taste better than they smell*'?"

Mom swatted at her. "Very funny."

Saturday morning, Cleo packed her backpack with everything she needed: floss, a beach towel, tacks, tape, and a big rolled-up banner with the name of her business. The only thing missing was her Extractor Extraordinaire!™ She went to find it.

Mom came out of the boys' room. Her hair looked like a raccoon nest. Dark shadows circled her eyes. "Julian's sick," she said. "I've been up with him all night. Sorry, honey, but there's no way we're going to the park."

Josh came bounding up the stairs. "Chocolate chip pancakes are ready! But don't give any to JayJay. I don't want to see what *that* looks like coming back up!"

Cleo ignored her brother's grossness. "Can Josh and I still go?"

"By yourselves?" Mom shook her head. "No, I don't think so." She headed toward the stairs.

Cleo followed on her heels. "*What?* Mom, I *have to go*! Customers will be expecting me. If I don't show, I'll lose people's trust. We'll just be at the park. It's not that far away." She was not giving up. "I'll take your cell phone. I'll wash the dishes for a month. We're test marketing your cookies! Remember?"

"I want to go!" Josh cried. "Emilio's coming."

Dad held out a huge platter of pancakes. "Breakfast is served!"

"Dad, can you come to the park with us? Get your assistant to cover for you?"

"I can't bail on my team. But we could head there as soon as the game is over." He walked out of the kitchen with the platter.

Cleo trailed him to the table. "What time would that be?"

"I don't know, maybe eleven thirty?"

"My flyer says I'll be there from ten to two!" This was horriful!

"Sit down and start eating. Everyone thinks better when their blood sugar's level." He pulled Mom into the kitchen.

They came back a minute later. "We're going to let you go on your own," Dad said. "But you'll have Mom's phone and the dog with you." Barkley, lying in the living room, lifted his head. Cleo didn't think an obese dog would intimidate anyone, if that's what her parents were thinking. Plus, he was a black Lab, the friendliest breed around. Now, if he *sat* on someone, that could do some damage. Anyway, she wasn't going to argue. Whatever it took to get to the park.

"I'll come as soon as the game is done."

Cleo beamed. "Thanks, Dad."

Dad kissed them all good-bye and headed out.

A little while later, Cleo was still at the table, her pancakes barely touched. Normally, she'd have gobbled them, like Barkley with the avocados.

Mom put her hand to Cleo's forehead. "You're not getting sick too, are you?"

"No, no! I'm fine. Just ready to get to the park." She stood and swung her backpack onto her shoulders. "I'll have one of your breakfast cookies later. Come on, Josh! Time to go!"

Josh ran into the room, wearing his Dodgers hat and carrying the Nerf gun. Barkley did his best to keep up with him.

Mom put the cookies in the main section of Cleo's

backpack and zipped her phone into the outside pocket. She clipped Barkley onto the leash and handed it to Josh. "See you when you get home. Oh! I almost forgot." Mom disappeared for a moment. She came back with a box of latex gloves and a container of gauze patches. "I want you to use these. Taking risks is one thing. Avoiding blood-borne illness is another."

Cleo started to protest until she imagined herself wearing the gloves. Like an actual doctor. Yes. Gloves and gauze definitely added a professional touch. "Thanks, Mom."

They headed down the walkway to the gate. "Don't forget about the cookies!" Mom called.

"Don't worry, Mom." Cleo smiled over her shoulder. "I can sell *anything!*"

As Dad said, she could sell teeth to a crocodile.

But right then, it was time to sell *pulling* teeth.

CHAPTER 12

Grand Opening

Cleo spied it immediately. A square picnic table in front of a wooden arbor covered in vines. The perfect spot to set up shop. She and Caylee, who'd walked with them to the park, tacked the banner to the arbor while Josh and Barkley ran around on the playground. Cleo spread the beach towel on the table, then laid out her business tools: the floss, the gauze, the gloves, and, of course, the Extractor Extraordinaire!™. Finally, she set out the bag of cookies.

Caylee had made a sign-up sheet. So they'd have people's email addresses, she said. "Which could be used for future marketing, if you want. My dad does that with his car business."

"Of course! Plus, we'll need them for people who buy a recording. Great idea, C-O-O!" Cleo held up her hand and they slapped a high five. She put the clipboard with the sign-up sheet on the table. All set. Now all they needed were some customers.

They sat next to each other on one of the benches attached to the table. Cleo admired Caylee's camera, with all its fancy features. "My parents would *never* buy me something like this. They don't think I take care of my stuff. Plus, they couldn't afford it."

Caylee scoffed. "My dad just likes to spend money. My parents fought about it all the time."

Cleo glanced at the time on Mom's phone. *10:06.* What if no one showed! And after she had talked so confidently all around school? Lexie Lewis would love that.

To get her mind on something other than her archenemy, she showed her archfriend how to tie a piece of floss to a missile and create a slipknot at the end. They each did three. Now they were *really* ready.

Cleo's Quick and Painless Tooth Removal Service was open for business!

Her stomach felt queasy again. Maybe she was just hungry. "Want a breakfast cookie?"

Caylee said okay, and Cleo handed her a dense, lumpy mound. Caylee nibbled on her cookie. Cleo took a bite. *Not splendarvelous,* she thought, *but not horriful either.* She ate the whole thing in a few bites. Caylee set hers down on the towel just as Jimmy Ryerson jogged over waving some dollar bills.

Cleo jumped up and went around to the front of the table.

"That YouTube video was so cool!" he said, putting his money on the table.

Cleo was glad Mom and Dad weren't there. She didn't know what she'd say if someone mentioned the video once Dad came.

"Hi, Jimmy. We're ready for you!" She picked up the Nerf gun but a sudden inspiration caused her to put it back down. "Actually . . . would you mind if we waited just a few minutes?"

"Why?"

"For PR purposes."

"PR?" Jimmy asked.

"Public relations."

Jimmy nodded as if he understood, but Cleo was pretty sure he didn't.

"We want to establish our reputation as a first-rate, professional, tooth-pulling service." He still looked clueless. "I want there to be a crowd."

Jimmy grinned. "The more people the better! As long as I get to go first."

"Absolutely!" She gave him back his money — for the moment. It wasn't good business to take payment before services had been performed.

They went to the playground and played a game of Lava Monster with a few other kids who were there. Jimmy ran around the jungle gym, which looked like a small castle, roaring and swiping at the kids, trying to nab them without coming all the way onto the structure. It was like tag, with the added excitement of a monster climbing the walls and a moat full of molten lava keeping the players from being able to escape the playground. If you got tagged, you entered the lava pit and became a lava monster too. The game continued until all had been caught.

At one point, Jimmy tripped over Barkley, who had been too slow to get out of his way. Jimmy writhed on the ground while Barkley's slobbery tongue lapped his face. "Get this dog off me!" he yelled. "He's licking me to death!"

The other kids laughed and cheered Barkley for getting the lava monster.

When Jimmy finally got to his feet, he had only one thing to say: "That dog's breath is *deadly*!"

They started up the game again. Cleo ignored the sick feeling in her stomach, even though it seemed to be getting worse. She played dangerously, taunting the lava monster from the edges of the equipment. Jimmy snagged her leg and she jumped into the lava pit. She climbed up and down the rope ladder and slides, trying to snatch the back of a squealing kid's shirt or the heel of a shoe. Barkley bounded around the structure, barking at all the excitement.

Tessa and Steffy had come as promised — they ran around, trying not to get caught. Emilio was there too, saying he had a loose tooth to be pulled. Cleo recognized a handful of other kids from school, not in her class. She hoped they were all there to get their teeth pulled.

It was time. She clambered to the top of the tallest slide, ignoring Steffy's complaints that she was over-stepping Lava Monster boundaries.

"Hey, everyone!" she yelled. "If you have a loose tooth you want pulled, Cleo's Quick and Painless Tooth Removal Service is now officially open for business!" She slid down the slide to the rubbery black turf. "And we're giving away free cookies!"

That got everyone's attention. Some kids even whooped with excitement. Barkley trotted alongside Josh and the rest of the kids to Cleo's table. A few adults wandered over, probably parents of customers.

Jimmy had sprinted to get there first. He picked up the Nerf gun and thrust it into the air. "I'm ready!"

Cleo pushed her way through the crowd. "Don't

touch anything! The Extractor Extraordinaire is for tooth pulling only!" She sucked in her breath at a sudden stabbing pain in her gut.

Jimmy set the Nerf gun down and held up his hands. "Okay, okay. Don't freak out."

She snapped on her latex gloves and loaded a missile. "You want it recorded, right?"

He nodded. "I'm going to put it on YouTube, just like Little Man over there!" He pointed to Josh, who beamed and waved at the crowd.

"Oh, and everyone who has a tooth pulled gets a picture with Josh, the boy in the video!" Cleo announced. "No extra charge."

Cleo nodded to Caylee, who got her camera in position. She pulled Jimmy a little ways away from the crowd, but not too far. She wanted everyone to be able to see her tooth-pulling method, live and in person. "Which one is it?"

Jimmy pointed to his lower left canine.

She slipped the floss around his tooth, tightened it, and held the Extractor in firing position. "Everyone, count down with me!" she shouted, getting caught up in the excitement of having her first official customer. "In five, four, three" — Jimmy tensed next to her — "two, one —"

POP!

Jimmy flinched. The tooth flew behind the missile like a streaking comet's tail. Some kids cheered. A couple of the adults clapped. It had worked!

Cleo tried to hand Jimmy a wad of gauze, but he was too busy finding and untying his tooth. He came back holding it above his head. "Woo-hoo! It didn't even hurt!"

Cleo couldn't have asked for a better testimonial. She glanced at Caylee to make sure she was getting all this. She was. This was actually going to work!

Jimmy finally calmed down enough to stick the gauze in his new hole, pay Cleo her three dollars, and pose for a picture with Josh. When they were done, Cleo handed him a cookie. Others held out their hands, so she went ahead and gave them cookies as well.

"Disgusting!" Jimmy hollered. "What's in these things?"

Uh-oh. The cookies might be a tougher sell than she'd thought. Their stock had just dropped precipitously.

"Anise," she said. "Licorice flavor." They'd tasted okay, but remembering their taste and texture gave her a sudden urge to throw up.

"Anise?" His face scrunched in disgust. "You mean, *anus*! These cookies taste like butt!" He hucked the solid mound over the arbor. Another boy did the same. Two or three dropped theirs on the ground. Barkley hungrily gobbled them up.

"Thanks for yanking my tooth, though!" Jimmy ran off, passing Dad, who walked toward them on the asphalt trail.

Cleo started to call for the next customer, but the words caught in her mouth. She doubled over and lost *her* cookies all over the pavement. The crowd scattered. "Ew!" "Gross!" "She ralphed!" "Let me out of here!"

Only Caylee, Tessa, and Steffy stayed. Even Josh ran off. Barkley sniffed at the vomit.

"Barkley, no!" Dad commanded. He said something

to a couple of parents who'd come over to help —
something about being her dad.

Cleo straightened, feeling dizzy and light-headed.
Dad and Caylee held her steady. "You're early," Cleo
whispered.

"Looks like I got here just in time. I was able to
break away before the game ended. The team understood, and they were up, four to zero."

"Are you okay, Cleo?" Tessa asked. Steffy's forehead was wrinkled with concern.

Cleo took a breath, trying to focus her eyes. "I
think so. Do you want your canines pulled?" She
looked at Tessa hopefully.

Tessa glanced around at the others. "Uh —"

"Sorry, boss," Dad said. "Time to close up shop."

Cleo felt too awful to argue. Too pukey to per-
suade. "Yeah, I guess so." She watched from the bench
as Tessa and Steffy took down the banner. Caylee
put everything in the backpack. Then Dad drove
them home.

CHAPTER 13

A Minor Setback

Cleo spent the rest of the weekend on the couch, watching recordings of *Fortune* with a trash can nearby, just in case. Mom and Josh got the bug too, so Dad ended up being nurse, cook (although no one felt like eating much), and janitor all weekend long. Barkley took turns in their rooms, lying on the floor near their beds.

Church was not an option Sunday morning. And they had to cancel their visit with Melanie, the boys' first mom. Usually, it was the other way around.

Melanie may have been flaky, but Cleo liked her. She always brought Cleo a little gift along with whatever she brought for the boys — a coin purse or a beaded bracelet or a headband.

Sunday night, after everyone was in bed, Josh appeared at Cleo's door, his Superman blankie draped over his arm. "I can't sleep."

Cleo lifted her head, not the tiniest bit sleepy. She'd been thinking about her business. "Come on." She pulled back her covers. He slipped in beside her and snuggled close.

Cleo had shared a room with Josh after they'd gotten him and JayJay from foster care, before the house add-on was done. She had just turned six. Josh was not yet two. He cried every night, it seemed, sucking his Superman blankie until the thing was half soaked. He would often end up in her bed, rubbing her hair between his fingers until he went back to sleep. It had made her feel good to be the big sister helping her new brother feel a little less scared.

He couldn't rub her sleep cap–covered braids, but

he didn't seem to want to. She heard him sucking on his thumb. She didn't try to stop him, even though the dentist had warned that if he didn't, there'd be permanent damage to his teeth. At least he didn't do it publicly, like JayJay.

"Why didn't Melanie want us anymore?"

Cleo felt a pit in her stomach. It was a horrible, awful question that she wished didn't have to be asked, or answered, even though she knew the right thing to say.

"It's not that she didn't *want* you, Joshy. She just couldn't keep you."

"But why?"

"She couldn't take care of you and JayJay the way you needed. I know it's hard. But if you hadn't come, I wouldn't have two great brothers. And that would be horriful."

She heard the pop of his thumb being released from his lips. "And I wouldn't have you." He turned his head, looking up at her with his big cow eyes. "That would be horriful too."

Her heart squeezed in her chest, and she hugged her brother tighter. If only it were as easy to answer the same question for herself as it was to answer Josh — and if only the answer she'd given him were enough to satisfy her questions as well.

She *was* glad she had Josh and JayJay and her parents. But sometimes she felt like a piggy bank without a stopper — no matter how much money got put in, it was never filled up. Would it always feel this way?

Monday morning, Cleo awoke alone. She wished her stomach still hurt and her body was still hot with a fever, but neither was true. She felt totally normal. And hungry. But she *did not* want to go to school. The story of how she'd gotten sick at the park would spread like a virus, and she would be reminded of her business failure over and over again.

Mom came in, took her temperature, and told her to get ready for school.

"I still feel sick," Cleo whispered hoarsely.

"You're fine, honey. Clearly, it was a twenty-four-hour bug. Now, get up and let's go. I'll give you a ride."

"And Caylee?"

"If she wants one."

Before getting ready, Cleo searched her room for her backpack. She'd been so out of it on Saturday she hadn't seen where Dad had put it. She found the bag in her closet, everything from Saturday still inside, including the Nerf gun and Mom's breakfast cookies. With all of them being so sick, Josh hadn't remembered his gun, and Mom hadn't asked how the cookies had gone over. Cleo hated to have to break it to her that they'd flopped.

When it was time to go, she left her backpack as it was, telling herself that she was bringing the Extractor just in case. Maybe she could pull the teeth of a few customers before school and get the focus back on her fun business idea, instead of on how she'd gotten sick at everyone's feet.

She would even try again with the cookies. If

Jimmy hadn't overreacted, the other kids might have eaten them.

She and Mom had both experienced minor PR setbacks, but she could fix that.

Cleo and Caylee sat in the rear of the minivan. Cleo talked excitedly about the professional organizer she'd seen on *Fortune*. "That's what you're going to do when you grow up, Caylee. You would be *perfect* at that job! Did you know you could make a career out of organizing?"

Caylee shook her head, looking mystified.

"I'd hire you," Mom said. "Our house needs some serious help in that department."

Cleo felt a spark of excitement. "That could be another business! Cleo and Caylee's Closet Clean-up!"

Mom glanced over her shoulder. "I'm not sure you're as qualified in the areas of cleaning and organizing as your friend."

Cleo rolled her eyes, even though Mom was right.

"That's a catchy business name, though," Mom said. "Speaking of which, how'd it go with the breakfast cookies? And do you have a name for them?"

"Not yet." Cleo hoped she wouldn't ask more.

"And the test marketing?"

Cleo smacked her lips. She took a breath. "Well . . . since I didn't really get to hand them out on Saturday, I thought I'd take them to school today." She paused. "If that's okay with you."

"Sure. Although they're a few days old. They may not be as good."

Cleo didn't have the heart to tell her it probably wouldn't make a difference. "I didn't think they were so bad."

Mom eyed her in the rearview mirror. "'Nicki's Breakfast Cookies: *They're not so bad.*' Hmm, I don't know . . . I think it's missing something."

Cleo turned to her friend. Caylee had barely said a word since she'd shown up at their house. "You okay?"

Caylee looked out the window. Were her eyes watering? Cleo sat silently, not sure what to say. Mom and the boys started singing "Down at the Station."

Caylee sniffled. "Yeah, I'm okay."

"What's wrong?"

She shrugged. "My dad made me go shopping on Rodeo Drive yesterday."

She'd been shopping on *Rodeo Drive* and she was crying? "Oh my gosh! I would so *die* to be taken shopping there."

Caylee gave her a sour look. "He brought his new *you-know-what*."

"Oh."

"Like I even care about expensive clothes."

Cleo swallowed. "Yeah." They were quiet the rest of the way.

Once they got to school, Caylee had more to share. "So, there's more bad news — I just didn't want to say it in the car."

Cleo spotted Tessa crossing the street. She grabbed Caylee's arm. "Can it wait? Customer — two o'clock."

She raised her eyebrows and motioned with her head in the direction of their friend.

Caylee's forehead bunched and her eyes got all blinky. Cleo didn't have time to deliberate. "Tessa!" she shouted, and waved. Were her loose teeth still in her mouth? If so, Cleo was going to offer to pull them, right then and there. Tessa could pay her later, if necessary. Her friend waved back but then stopped to wait for Steffy, who was coming along the sidewalk.

Cole Lewis walked up. "Where were you Saturday? I came at one and you weren't there."

"Ohhh." Cleo stalled. She glanced at Caylee, who stood there looking flustered. What was the big deal? He was just a *boy*. "I had a little . . . problem. We had to close early."

"Oh. Okay." He was about to walk away. She could feel it. "Funny video, though," he said, turning to leave.

"Wait a second." She grabbed him. He looked down at her hand squeezing his arm. "Sorry," she said, laughing a little. She let go.

He brushed off his sleeve with the tops of his fingers.

Cleo regained her composure. "I can do it *now*. Before school starts." She looked around the playground for a good spot. A spot where the recess monitor wouldn't see them. "Behind the portable!" she exclaimed.

Cole looked startled. "Wow. You don't mess around, do you?"

No, she didn't. Not when she had a chance to clean up her PR mess. If Big Man of the Classroom Cole Lewis used her service, loads of kids would be lining up to do the same. She'd be back in business for sure!

Caylee pulled her off to the side. "Did you bring the Nerf gun to school?" she whispered urgently.

"It's okay," Cleo whispered back. How had she managed to surround herself with such worrywarts? She held up her pointer finger to Cole and mouthed the words, "Just a sec."

"It's just one extraction, Jelly. It'll be super quick. No one will even see us."

"Cleo, you *can't*. You can get in *serious* trouble."

Cole had his arms crossed. "Excuse me, are you done with your little meeting?"

Cleo hurried back to her customer. Caylee huffed and walked in the opposite direction. "I won't be able to video it," Cleo said.

"I don't care."

"Do you have a dollar?"

"Fifty cents."

"Fifty cents!"

"That's all I've got. Milk money."

Cleo pursed her lips. "Okay. Fifty cents. *And* you become my company's official spokesperson."

Cole stroked his chin. "You got a deal." He stuck out his hand and they shook. "The first person I'm going to send your way is my sister. She's driving my family *nuts* with all her whining." He jumped around on his toes, flapping his hands and making his voice go high. "'Ooo, ooo, my tooth! I can't eat! I can't brush my teeth!'" He put his hands on his cheeks and pulled down, exposing the pink skin inside his lower eyelids. "'It hu-u-u-rts.'"

Cleo laughed at his impersonation of Lexie. She was about to suggest they go do business when Tessa and Steffy walked up. "Oh my gosh, Cleo. Are you all right?" Tessa asked.

"You were so sick!" Steffy added.

"I'm fine. Thanks for, uh, asking." She smiled nervously at Cole, who looked at her suspiciously. "Tessa! Do you still have your canines?"

"Yeah. I was hoping you'd pull them out for me."

"Perfect! Follow me!" Cleo bounded toward the portable. As soon as they were out of sight of everyone on the playground, she put her pack on the ground, got a missile ready, and loaded her Extractor Extraordinaire!™. "You can pay me later, Tessa," she told her friend.

Within a matter of minutes, she had sent three teeth flying. Afterward, Cole gave Tessa a fist bump. "You are one tough girl," he said. She grinned, wads of gauze stuffed in her holes. The whistle blew.

Cole gave Cleo a fist bump too. She held open her hand. "I think you owe me something else as well."

"I was going to give it to you!" he said, reaching into his pocket. He placed two quarters on her palm.

"Oh! And I have something for you too." She opened the bag of cookies. "My mom offered them as a gift to my customers."

Tessa just squinted and said, "No thanks." Steffy also declined.

"I'll have one," Cole said. "I never turn down cookies." He took a bite. His face contorted and he spit it out. "Don't give these to your customers. They won't come back!"

Steffy and Tessa nodded, their faces apologetic.

Cole dropped the cookie on the ground. "Maybe a squirrel or bird will want it. But I doubt it."

Poor Mom. Back to the drawing board for her.

As soon as they got into their room, Cole started grandstanding about the hole in his mouth. He paraded around, holding up his molar. "Yes, I am a proud client of Cleo's Quick and Painless Tooth-Pulling —"

"Removal," Cleo corrected.

"Huh?" Cole looked confused.

"It's Cleo's Quick and Painless Tooth *Removal* Service."

"Oh. Right. Anyway, it was quick, but it hurt like crazy!" He held his cheek. "It's still throbbing. Ow."

Cleo glared at him.

"Just joking. I barely felt a thing!" He chortled. A real comedian, that kid.

"When did you pull *his* tooth?" Jimmy asked.

Cleo glanced at Caylee. She looked away.

"I thought you'd shut down your business after you lost your lunch on the sidewalk." Jimmy laughed. Several kids groaned.

Mr. Boring's duck call quacked. "Okay, okay. That's enough. So, Cleo, I've been wondering all weekend, how'd it go?"

"She had to take a sick day!" Jimmy called out.

"Jimmy . . . ," Mr. Boring warned.

Cleo lifted her chin. "It's true. But I'm back in business. Tessa is another of my satisfied customers."

Tessa grinned, showing off two big gaps. Cleo's stock was on the rise again.

CHAPTER 14

A Perfect Opportunity

Cleo had to chase Caylee down at first recess. She found her at the tetherball pole, waiting to play either Tessa or Lexie Lewis, depending on who won. She elbowed Caylee. "I told you it would be okay." Caylee didn't return her smile.

Lexie pounded the ball, around and around.

"You're really good at that!" Cleo shouted above the sounds of the game. *Whap! Whizzzz. Clang!*

"Thanks, LeSnore!" *Whap! Whizzzz. Clang!*

Cleo didn't have time to get mad. She was working

Fortune Principle Number Seven: *Compliments win customers.* She hadn't forgotten her goal of winning Lexie Lewis's business. And now she knew for a fact that she *did* have a loose tooth in that big mouth of hers.

The last of the rope coiled around the pole. "Tether!" Lexie looked at Cleo out of the corner of her eye. "You playing?" It sounded like a challenge.

"Caylee was here first."

Lexie unwound the ball. Caylee took Tessa's spot. Lexie served the ball above Caylee's head and it wrapped around the pole — *one* — around again — *two* — Lexie slapped it — *three* . . . If Caylee didn't get the ball soon, she would be through. Lexie lost her balance, and Caylee whacked it back. *Boom!* Around again. *Boom!*

Cleo had never seen her best friend go after a ball like that. Caylee scowled and pounded the ball — *Boom!* She was like a heavyweight boxer hitting someone she really didn't like.

"Time out!" Lexie called. She reached down as if she'd dropped something on the ground. Just as she stood, Caylee hammered the ball again — double fisted. The ball smashed right into Lexie's face!

"Owwww!" Lexie's hands flew to her face.

"Oh no!" Caylee cried. "I'm so sorry!"

"I have an audition for a TV commercial tomorrow!" Lexie screeched from behind her hands.

"I didn't mean to —" Caylee rushed over. She reached out but Lexie shrugged her off.

"If you broke my nose, I'll . . . I'll have my dad sue your dad!"

Caylee looked at her blankly.

"It's going to be swollen! I can tell! If I don't get that part, it'll be *your* fault."

"You *should* get the part." Cleo crossed her arms. "Because you sure know how to act."

"Butt out, LeSnore!"

"She didn't even hit you that hard."

Lexie lowered her hands, peering into them. Was she looking for a tooth? Fortune Principle Number Five popped into Cleo's head: *A visionary sees opportunities everywhere — especially in crises.* This crisis was a *perfect* opportunity! "Is your mouth okay?" she asked.

"I think it's bleeding," Lexie moaned.

Cleo got closer. "Let me look."

Lexie eyed her cautiously.

"It's okay. I know first aid."

Lexie opened her mouth. Cleo had to stand on her toes to see inside. "There's some blood around one of your teeth. I think it might be loose."

Lexie held her cheek and groaned.

"A loose tooth. Hmmm . . ." Cleo tapped her lips with her finger, then held the finger in the air. "I know just the place you could go to have it removed. Tessa has used our service with stunning results. Am I right, Tessa?"

Tessa bared her teeth, revealing her gaps.

"No!" Lexie started toward the building. "I'm not going to use your stupid business."

Cleo caught up with her. "My business is *not* stupid. It really works! I'm offering a special — today only. Fifty cents a tooth!"

Lexie kept walking. Cleo stayed with her. "Just give it a try!" She grabbed Lexie's arm.

"Get your hands off me, you freak."

"I am not a freak!"

"Why *else* would your mom give you away?" She tossed the question over her shoulder, lightly, as if she were talking about clothes that had gotten too small.

Her words hit Cleo like a sucker punch to the gut. Anger twisted her insides like a tornado. She lashed out with her fists, not even sure who or what she was hitting. The tornado had control of her arms and legs. She would claw and kick and punch until all of the anger and hurt were gone. But the more she hit, the worse she felt.

Someone screamed. It might have been herself. Or was it Lexie? Maybe it was the blur of kids who had come around. She felt a firm grip on her elbow, heard Mr. Boring's voice in her ear. "Calm down, Cleo."

She breathed as hard as if she'd just run laps with Dad's soccer team. Her knuckles hurt.

Lexie sat on the ground, sobbing, her face in her hands.

Cole crouched at his sister's side. Another teacher was there, helping her up.

Lexie cried out. "My tooth! It's gone! *She knocked my tooth out!*"

Everyone stared. A few kids started looking around on the ground. Micah Mitchell shouted, "Here it is!" and handed the tooth to Lexie. She glared at Cleo as the teacher led her away.

"It was already loose," Cleo pleaded to Mr. Boring. She needed her teacher to understand. He said they needed to go to the office.

She looked around for Caylee, but Caylee stayed where she was, in a huddle of girls, only once glancing in Cleo's direction.

"Hey!" Cole trotted up. "I know my sister can be a pain, but you didn't have to go all MMA on her."

Cleo tried to say "sorry," but she was afraid she might cry.

Mr. Boring looked serious. He nudged her forward. "Come on, Cleo. Let's get inside."

It suddenly dawned on Cleo. She was in a lot of trouble.

She spent the rest of the morning in the office, first waiting until Lexie had seen the nurse, then sitting in front of Principal Yu, talking about what had happened.

"My dad is a lawyer. He'll sue you for damages," Lexie threatened. She had suddenly gained a lisp, as if her tongue didn't know what to do with the new gap in her mouth.

"Hold on, now." Principal Yu leaned forward in his chair. "Nurse Bishara said she didn't see any injuries — just your tooth, which I've been told was loose already."

Thank you, Mr. Boring.

"So. Girls. What happened out there?" Mr. Yu pushed his black-rimmed glasses farther up on his nose.

"She attacked me!"

"Cleo, do New Heights Eagles use hitting to solve problems?" He stared at Cleo, unblinking. Cleo felt herself getting warmer, as if Principal Yu's gaze had fire-starting power.

"No, Mr. Yu." She kept her eyes on her lap, wishing he would stop staring at her.

"No, they don't. New Heights Eagles talk it out. And if it's too big a problem to resolve on their own, they get an adult."

Lexie crossed her arms. "She was pestering me to use her tooth-pulling business." She moved like a bobble-head toy, her head swiveling on her neck as she spoke. "She pulls teeth with a Nerf gun. She did it to my brother before school — behind the portable. She's *obsessed!*"

Principal Yu's eyebrows rose. "A Nerf gun? Behind the portable?"

Meat loaf and McDonald's.

"Actually . . ." Cleo needed to speak up before Lexie Lewis had her convicted and on her way to jail — or rather, suspension. "It was for a class project — my Passion Project!"

"Your passion is pulling teeth?" Mr. Yu looked at her over the top of his glasses.

"No!" Cleo laughed. *Silly Principal Yu.* "Starting *businesses!* I got the idea for a tooth removal service when one of my friends was afraid to pull her own teeth. I have an ad on YouTube if you want to see." Cleo leaned forward excitedly.

Mr. Yu pushed back his chair. "Maybe later. Please stay here, ladies." He left his office.

Lexie Lewis smiled smugly.

Cleo drummed her fingers on her thighs. *Was she in trouble for the Nerf gun, or not?*

A few minutes later, Mr. Yu came back with Mr. Boring. Cleo's heart sank.

Mr. Boring took the seat next to Cleo. "Cleo, did you bring a Nerf gun to school?" His eyes were kind, but she knew the answer would seriously disappoint him.

She looked at her hands in her lap. "Yes, Mr. Boring." Her head snapped up. "But I wasn't playing with it. And I wasn't hurting anyone. I just" — she glanced at Principal Yu — "pulled a few loose teeth, that's all."

Principal Yu sucked in his breath. "I'm sorry, Miss Oliver, but between initiating a fight with Miss Lewis —"

She's the one who started it! Cleo wanted to shout.

"— and bringing a gun to school —"

"Not a *gun*, Mr. Yu. My Extractor Extraordinaire (trademark)!"

Lexie scoffed under her breath.

"— and bringing a *gun* to school, I'm going to have to send you home for the day as a consequence of your poor choices."

"Mr. Yu," Mr. Boring spoke, "if I may interject for just a moment, do we know what prompted the, uh, outburst?" He turned to Cleo. "Why did you hit Lexie?"

Cleo's palms were suddenly clammy. Her heart beat so hard it shook her chest. She needed to get away. To go *home*.

Principal Yu turned to her. "Miss Oliver?"

Telling Mr. Yu what Lexie had said would be like Barkley exposing his belly. He only did that with family.

"Miss Oliver?"

She couldn't repeat the words. "She was making fun of me because I'm adopted."

Principal Yu cleared his throat. "I'm very sorry to hear that." His blowtorch gaze landed squarely on Lexie. "Miss Lewis, is being adopted something to make fun of?"

Lexie huffed. "I guess not."

"You guess not?" His face was turning red.

"No, it's not."

"Girls, I'll be talking to your parents and teachers about further actions in light of today's incident. Now, you need to apologize to each other."

Apologizing was surely the *last* thing in the world that Cleo wanted to do, but she knew there was no escaping it. "I'm . . . sorry." The words came out pinched and tight, like money being pulled from a miserly person's hand.

Lexie barely glanced at her. "Sorry." She said it like a knife jab.

Mr. Yu pushed up his glasses again. "Miss Lewis, please return to class."

Lexie put her hand to her mouth and winced in pain. She gave a little sob, then sulked from the room, an excellent performance.

"Miss Oliver, will one of your parents be able to pick you up?" Mr. Yu asked.

Cleo gasped. "I still have to go home?" She'd thought what she'd told him about Lexie would change his mind.

He nodded once.

"My mom," she said, avoiding Mr. Boring's gaze.

"I'll call now. You may wait in the main office." He and Mr. Boring exchanged glances. "Thank you, Mr. Boring."

Mr. Boring's name suddenly struck Cleo as funny. Coming from Mr. Yu's serious mouth it was hilarious. Hysterical. *Hilaristerical.* She couldn't stop giggling.

Mr. Boring led her to the row of chairs along the front window. He sat next to her. "What's so funny?"

She looked up at him. "Your name!" She sputtered and laughed some more.

Thankfully, Mr. B was laughing with her. "Your tooth-pulling method is brilliant, by the way."

"Thanks, Mr. B, but I have a feeling I won't be using it again anytime soon." If only she hadn't gotten so worked up about Lexie's stupid words, maybe she wouldn't be unemployed.

CHAPTER 15
Horriful Times a Hundred

"What happened?" Mom wanted to know as soon as Cleo was in the van.

"She deserved it," Cleo said, slamming the side door shut. Why couldn't they have a *nice* minivan with the doors that quietly slid themselves closed at the push of a button?

Mom turned in her seat to look at Cleo. "I know she said something about you being adopted. It must have been pretty bad for you to hit her in the mouth."

"You hit a girl?" JayJay said with awe. "Why did you hit a *girl*?"

"If a boy had said what Lexie Lewis said, I would have hit a boy."

"What did she say?" Mom asked.

"Can we talk about it later?" Cleo clutched her backpack to her chest.

Mom sighed, giving her that *Disappointed Mom* look that made her feel all broken up inside. "All right. But you're not wiggling out of this one, Cleo. You *will* tell me." Mom eyed her in the rearview mirror. "And the Nerf gun? Cleo! What were you thinking?"

She wanted to say, *Sometimes you can't think — you just need to trust your instincts.* But in this case, a little more thinking probably would've been a good idea.

After lunch, Cleo took her backpack to the kitchen. She made sure the coast was clear and then she dumped "Nicki's Breakfast Cookies: *Everyone thinks they're disgusting*" in the tall trash can, being sure to cover them up. She rinsed out the baggie — Mom

was a fanatic about not adding to the global landfill —
and put it in the drying rack. Then she realized seeing
the baggie might remind Mom to ask about the
cookies, and she didn't want to have to break it to her
just *how* badly they'd flopped, so she stuffed the plastic bag in the trash too, being *extra* sure to cover
that up.

Then she went to her room and shut the door. She
dragged her desk chair over to the closet. If she stood
on her tippy toes, she could reach high enough. She
pulled down the flat white box and set it on her bed.
She took the chair to the door and jammed it under
the doorknob.

She sat on her bed and placed the box on her lap.
She took off the lid and lifted out the little outfit
inside. A lavender top with eight sewn-on orange butterflies. Lavender pants with satin orange ruffles
around the bottoms. They looked like doll clothes,
they were so small. This was what she'd been wearing
the day her parents had gotten her. Clothes from her
birth mom. Purple and orange. Her and Fortune's
favorite colors.

Underneath the lavender-and-orange outfit was a pink ruffly dress with pink ruffly underpants. This one was from the foster mom. In the one picture Cleo had seen of herself wearing it, she was bawling. She didn't blame herself. The dress was horrific times a *hundred*.

She searched for the little plastic bag and plucked it out from among the ruffles. She admired the sparkly gold chain with the shiny heart pendant. She stood in front of the mirror on her closet door and held the tiny heart earrings up to her ears. Mom didn't want her ears pierced. Maybe when she turned eleven, she said. Cleo bugged her about it constantly, but so far, Persuasion Power™ hadn't gotten her anywhere with this one.

She took out the necklace and put it on. It was something she did every once in a while — not a whole lot, but sometimes.

It was hard to think about her. This person known only as her "birth mom."

She was African American–Filipino (which meant Cleo had relatives all the way over in the Philippines —

in Asia!). She had been a college student when she got pregnant. Cleo's birth father was African American. And that's pretty much all Cleo knew.

The lavender outfit, the jewelry, and Beary, the floppy purple bear that she slept with every night, were all she had of her. Her birth mom had left them with Cleo when she handed her over.

Why else would your mom give you away?

She tried not to think it, but the question kept repeating, as if Lexie Lewis were inside her head, mocking her over and over.

She stood on her bed. She put the side of her face against Fortune, trying to imagine it was soft and warm, but it wasn't. It was just some paper on a wall. An ache so deep it went all the way to the bottoms of her feet caused her eyes to water.

She looked through bleary eyes at Fortune's radiant face. She had wanted to believe *this* woman was her birth mom. Tried so hard to believe it. And she'd made what this woman had done okay by thinking she'd *had* to place her for adoption. Because she was destined to be *Fortune* and she couldn't let *anything* stop her, not even a baby.

But it was a fantasy. It was *only* a fantasy.

She ripped the poster from the wall and tossed it to the ground.

Mom and Dad always talked about it like it was such a brave and loving thing her birth mom had done, recognizing she couldn't give Cleo the home she deserved. But at this particular moment, Cleo wasn't buying it.

If her birth mom had known what a great kid Cleo would become, she would have *found* a way to keep her close. Cleo crawled under her comforter and hugged Beary to her chest. She didn't try to keep herself awake.

Someone was knocking on her door. Dad called her name. Cleo looked at the clock on her nightstand. 2:38. Dad was home already?

She shuffled across the floor, rubbing her eyes. She removed the chair and opened the door.

"Cleo, what have I told you about blocking your —" Mom's eyes went to the chain around Cleo's neck. "You got down the things from your birth mom."

Cleo turned away. She quickly gathered the baby outfits, stuffed them back in the box, and shut them in her closet. She left the necklace on.

"Don't you have soccer?" she asked Dad.

"My assistant's covering for me."

Mom picked up the poster of Fortune. "Why's this on the ground?"

"I took it down."

Mom peered into her face. She set the poster on Cleo's desk. "Sweetie, what's going on?" She led Cleo to the bed and they sat. "What did that girl say to you?"

Dad pulled up her desk chair.

Josh's face appeared around the door frame. "Did Cleo get kicked out of school?"

"She had a hard day," Dad said, heading for the

door. "You and Jay play in your room for a bit. I'll come in a few minutes."

Josh sped off.

As soon as the door was shut, Cleo spilled it all. Caylee accidentally hitting Lexie with the tetherball. Cleo seeing the bloody loose tooth in Lexie's mouth. How she'd tried to convince Lexie to let her pull it. "I guess I got a little pushy."

"You?" Dad said, smiling.

"Then she called me a freak."

"And so you *hit* her?" Mom suddenly didn't sound so understanding.

"No. I told her I wasn't a freak."

Dad nodded. "That sounds like a good response."

"Then *she* said, 'Why else would your mom give you away?'"

Mom inhaled sharply. She put her arm around Cleo, as if to protect her from what had been said. Her eyes sparked. "Oh honey, I am so sorry." She lifted Cleo's chin. "Listen to me. You *know* there is nothing wrong with being adopted."

Cleo nodded, although she still wished she hadn't had to be.

"And you have no reason to be ashamed. It's that girl . . . what's her name?"

"Lexie Lewis."

"*Lexie Lewis* should be ashamed of herself, and she *will* be after I get ahold of her. She will rue the day she met Cleopatra's mother." Cleo had no idea what *rue* meant, but if it had anything to do with being sorry, then Cleo rued the day she had met Lexie Lewis.

"Nicki, calm down a minute." Dad put his heavy hand on Cleo's leg. "It's understandable you were angry," Dad said. "You were hurt. But it's not okay that you took it out on Lexie the way you did."

"I know. I just lost it. I think I understand better how Josh feels when he goes berserk. I'm really sorry."

"Does Lexie know that?"

Cleo bit the side of her mouth. "I apologized. Kind of."

Dad looked at her tenderly. "I know you'll find a

way to make it right with her. Now" — Dad crossed his arms — "as for the Nerf gun . . . you knew you were breaking a rule when you brought that to school, didn't you?"

"Yeah." She searched for the words that would make *that* part of her actions right, but she was having a hard time finding them. It had been a dumb risk. "I guess I just wanted to make up for Saturday going so badly."

Dad nodded. "Hmmm."

She might as well tell them now about the video of Josh — get all the punishments over with at once. "And there's more bad news." The phrase jogged her memory. Caylee had said the exact same thing that morning . . . but she couldn't remember what Caylee's bad news was.

"Go on . . ." Mom prompted.

"I used Dad's tablet to record me yanking Josh's tooth, then I put it on YouTube."

"You *what*?" Mom said.

"YouTube. The video-sharing website?"

"I know what it is, Cleo! I just can't believe . . . you know how to do that?" She looked astonished. Dad looked like he was trying not to smile.

"Actually, Ernie Junior, I mean, E.J., did it, but I know how to now!"

Mom scratched her forehead. She looked stumped. "I — I don't know what to say. I think I should be angry, but I'm not sure."

"It's already gotten almost eight hundred views!" Cleo announced, since Mom hadn't grounded her on the spot.

"Eight hundred?" Now it was Dad's turn to be astonished. "How —?"

"Probably because the link was on the flyer I handed out to everyone at school. My advertising worked!"

Dad crossed his arms. "Joshy went viral. Wow. Ooo! I'll show it to my students. That will definitely raise my cool quotient."

Cleo gave Dad a *Don't get your hopes up* look — arms crossed, one eyebrow raised, lips off to one side.

"Hold on." Mom sounded grave. Cleo slumped. She should have known Mom wouldn't let it pass so easily. Here came the consequence. "*I* want to see this YouTube hit first!" She wrapped her solid arms around Cleo. "I was bummed I missed the actual event. Thanks to you, we've got it recorded!"

Cleo relaxed, grateful for her real mom's *real* embrace.

"And if you're wondering — yes, there *will* be a consequence for taking your father's tablet without asking."

Oh well. At least she could count on her mom to be consistent.

CHAPTER 16

The Cookies Make
a Comeback

The whole family gathered around the computer to watch Josh and Cleo on YouTube. They watched it four times, laughing hysterically every time, especially during the slow-motion part. Cleo imitated Josh's yell, low and stretched out, sending JayJay into fits. Even Josh giggled.

Mom was in the middle of telling Cleo that although the video was very funny, she wouldn't be using the tablet for the rest of the month, when a loud crash came from the kitchen. Everyone froze.

"Barkley?" Mom called. He'd been watching with them but was nowhere in sight at the moment.

They hurried to the kitchen. Mom stopped in the doorway, jamming up traffic behind her. The tipped trash can had spewed garbage everywhere. "Barkley! Bad dog!"

Barkley wasn't listening. He was finding and gulping down Mom's breakfast cookies! He gobbled at least five of them before Mom grabbed him by the collar and pulled him away. "Hey, why are my cookies in the trash? Cleo, I thought you took these to school today."

Cleo stood frozen. Dad looked her in the eye.

Pizza and PepsiCo.

"I did," she said.

"Oh." Mom looked at the mess, the corners of her lips pulled down.

Dad put his arm around Mom. "Sorry, honey. Come on, gang, time to swab the decks!" Mom stooped to pick up some hot-dog packaging and a banana peel.

"Hey, at least *Barkley* loves them!" Cleo grinned at Mom, but she was too busy scraping up coffee grounds to notice. Barkley had his tail between his legs. He whimpered. Cleo knelt and looked into Barkley's eyes. "You made a *big* mess, boy. I know how you feel." She went to kiss his nose, but he licked her face first. His breath no longer had the horrible fishy stench. It smelled sweet. "Mom," she said, "I think your cookies have worked a miracle!"

Mom glanced up from some egg slime. Dad kept throwing stuff into the trash can. Conveniently, Josh and Julian had taken off. "What are you talking about?"

"Barkley's breath! It actually smells *good!*"

Cleo could see the lightbulb going on in Mom's head. "Oh, that's funny. I bet it's the anise. It's a natural breath freshener."

Dad came over and sniffed Barkley's mouth. "Mmm . . . not bad."

Now *Cleo* had a lightbulb moment. "Mom, I think you can sell these at the farmer's market after all!"

"I'm not sure a dog's testimonial is going to win many people over." Mom went back to the egg goo. "'They're irresistible: I even pawed through *garbage* for them. Woof!'"

Dad chuckled.

"Not people." Cleo felt her smile growing. "Dogs. You'd be selling them to *dogs.*" Her smile felt almost as wide as her face. "Well, to the owners of dogs, but they'd be *for* the dogs!"

For a second, Mom looked surprised — or maybe insulted, Cleo wasn't sure — then she threw back her head and laughed.

"And I know what we can call them," Cleo said. Her very enterprising mind was firing on all cylinders. "*Cleo's Canine Cookies!*" Mom laughed harder. She even snorted once.

"That's not bad," Dad said. "I like it."

"I'll help you sell them." She had another idea! "And what about my Canine Carrier Capsule (trademark)? We could sell those with them. We could even package them together! And I could write a training manual for how to teach your dog to carry messages, and —"

"Whoa, whoa. One thing at a time," Mom said. She went to the sink to wash her hands.

Barkley stood there panting — totally clueless about the great idea he had just inspired.

"We could make *real* money with this," Cleo said. "Then you wouldn't have to worry so much."

Mom's forehead wrinkled. "Worry?"

"About having enough to pay bills."

Mom and Dad looked at each other. "Oh, honey," Mom hugged her again. "Don't you worry about that. We'll be fine. God always provides."

They were quiet, and for a moment, Cleo felt like her piggy bank was full.

"I think you're onto something, Cleo," Dad said. "But there's one requirement."

"What?"

"Your mom and I become your board of directors." Dad picked up another Canine Cookie and tossed it to Barkley. The dog caught it midair and gobbled it down. "All decisions related to the running of your businesses get passed by us first — including any social media marketing campaigns." He smiled.

"Isn't the CEO usually the chairperson of the board?" Cleo asked.

Dad laughed. "Sometimes, yes, I believe so."

"All right, then. It's a deal. You'll be my board, and I'll be Chairgirl of the Board!"

CHAPTER 17

Some Fortunate Advice

"Hi, Cleo." Caylee had called her. "So . . . will you be at school tomorrow?"

Cleo sat on her bed, refolding the baby clothes from her birth mom so she could put them away properly. "I think so."

"What did Principal Yu say?"

"He said I had to go home."

Silence. Finally, Caylee spoke. "I've never seen you like that."

"Me neither."

"It kind of freaked me out."

"Me too."

"I'm sorry I didn't come over. I mean, after Mr. Boring . . . stopped you. It was just . . . well, I was sort of —"

"It doesn't matter. Hey, guess what? I've got another business idea!" Cleo had a sense she should be asking Caylee about her "more bad news," and she would — just as soon as she told her about Cleo's Canine Cookies™! She told her about the trash can incident and her happy discovery that Barkley's breath smelled good after eating a bunch of the cookies. "I was wondering if you'd take some shots of Barkley for the label. He's going to be the face of Cleo's Canine Cookies — and related products — and you're a *way* better photographer than me. My pictures always turn out blurry or off center, but not in a cool, artistic way like yours. Or the subjects look like zombies from Planet Doofus. Your shots always look inspired, like pieces of art! Plus, you've got that nice new camera."

Caylee sighed. "I —"

"Please, Jelly! Pretty please with a gummy pizza on top?"

"Okay."

"Great! Can we do it this afternoon? How about after *Fortune*? Ask your mom if you can come over and watch it with me. We'll take the pictures after that. Then you can eat dinner with us!" She was on a roll. "These dog cookies are going to be a huge hit, Caylee. I can *feel* it! This isn't a little tooth-pulling operation or selling fruit from our trees. This is going to be a real business, with real profits!"

More silence. Longer this time.

Cleo looked at the phone, then put it back to her ear. "Are you still there?"

"Is that all you can talk about?" Caylee suddenly sounded mad.

What had she done wrong? "What?"

"Business! Money! All you ever talk about are your businesses and how to make more money. Not everyone is into money like you are, you know."

"I'm not —"

"*I'm* not into money like you are."

"I — I thought you liked my ideas. You said you wanted to be my COO."

"Money isn't everything, Cleo. It doesn't make all your problems go away — and, and . . . it *can't* make up for a person not being there!" *Click.*

"Caylee?"

Had Caylee just *hung up* on her?

Cleo stared at the phone, waiting for her friend to call back, and then when she didn't, trying to figure out if she should call *her*. Okay, so money wasn't everything — she knew that — but it was still *something*. People needed money to live, to go to the doctor, to buy things for their kids. She looked at the little outfit on her lap. She traced a butterfly with her finger.

It can't make up for a person not being there.

Oh no. They were coming. And there was nothing she could do to stop them.

Tears. Hot, stinging, horriful tears.

She buried her face in the tiny baby clothes and bawled.

Cleo went downstairs when it was time for *Fortune*. Mom and Dad were talking in the family room. She could hear Josh and Jay playing outside with Barkley. She appeared in the doorway and her parents looked up.

"Everything okay?" Mom's eyes narrowed in concern.

Cleo didn't want to talk about her best friend hanging up on her, or any of the feelings that had come along with it. She would call Caylee back later, maybe after *Fortune*. "Would it be all right if I watched my show?" She wasn't sure if she was banished from TV, after all the trouble she'd been getting into.

"How about we watch it together?" Dad said.

Cleo broke into a smile. Dad never watched with her. Usually, he wasn't home, but he also said it was too cheesy for him. Dad clicked the remote and the

TV flickered to life. A commercial was on. He muted the sound.

She sat between her parents on the couch. Mom wrapped an arm around her shoulders and kissed her braided head.

"Did you know your dad and I consider ourselves to be two of the richest people on the planet?"

Cleo looked back and forth between them. She shook her head.

"Of course we do! Because we have you. And your brothers."

Josh and JayJay appeared at the windows, as if they'd heard Mom talking about them. They made goofy expressions, their faces plastered to the glass. Cleo and her parents laughed and made faces back. The boys ran off, chasing Barkley.

"Your birth mom didn't give you away, Cleo," Dad said. "She gave you to *us*."

"And what a gift." Mom squeezed Cleo. "What a *gift*."

Cleo felt like a gift, all wrapped up in her parents'

arms. And yet the question still tugged at her heart: *Why didn't my mom keep me?*

At least her parents had kept her name. That was something else she had from her birth mom. "I told Mr. Boring my birth mom named me Cleopatra, and he said I'll always be a queen in her eyes."

"Mr. Boring sounds like a smart man," Dad said.

"Do you know what 'Cleopatra' means?" Cleo asked, thinking about Anusha's *beautiful morning star.*

"As a matter of fact, I do," Dad said. "It means *glory of the father.*"

Cleo pondered the phrase. *Glory.* It made her think of those flowers . . . morning glories. She loved those. She wasn't exactly sure what glory was, but it was definitely something good.

"And what about Lenore?" Her parents had given her that part of her name after Gran Eleanor, who'd been named after a president's wife.

"Light," Mom said.

That was nice too. *Glory light.* She'd keep Edison for now, though.

"She wouldn't have named me Cleopatra if she thought I wasn't worth anything."

Mom's chin moved back and forth on top of Cleo's head. "No, she wouldn't have."

"Do you think she thinks about me?" Cleo whispered.

"All the time," Mom said.

"I think about her too. Not all the time. But a lot."

Her parents were quiet. Was it okay that she had said that?

"Of course you would," Dad said. "It's normal to wonder about where we come from."

"Do you think . . ." Cleo wasn't sure about this next part. Did she really want to do what she was about to ask?

Fortune's face appeared. "Dad, the sound!" Dad pointed the remote and Fortune's theme music bopped into the room.

Clips from past shows zoomed across the screen: Fortune laughing with singer-superstar Magdelena; Fortune putting her arm around an audience member;

Fortune hugging a girl in a wheelchair, talking into a microphone, blowing a kiss to the camera. Cleo reached up, grabbed the kiss, and slapped it onto her cheek, like always.

The camera panned the studio audience, then focused on Fortune, who wrapped her arms around herself as if the crowd's applause were a big hug. She wore a purple blazer speckled with white, as if she'd been dusted with powdered sugar. Her string of giant pearls matched her perfectly straight white teeth. Her shiny black hair was shellacked into place, and as always, she glowed.

"Hello, everyone! Thank you for being here. Thank you for *being*. I will never forget the day I discovered my purpose — to finance futures and deliver destinies. We all have a reason for being, so find your reason and —" She held out her hands to everyone.

"Live it!" Cleo shouted with the audience. She glanced at Mom and they exchanged big smiles.

Fortune loved to talk about people's "reason for being." At least once every show, it seemed, she'd say something about purpose or passion or destiny. "You know you have a purpose, right?" She looked out at the audience, and everyone shouted, "Yes!"

She said it again into the camera. "You know you have a purpose, right?"

"Yes!" Cleo shouted. Dad's eyebrows arced in surprise.

To be a high-climbing, heights-defying, limit-pushing entrepreneur. To start businesses. That was her purpose. Maybe one day she'd even do what Fortune had done and build schools in Africa. Not just schools . . . homes. Yes, she would build homes for kids who didn't have them, because every child needed somewhere to belong.

"When we come back, I'm going to introduce you to one determined young woman who refused to miss her calling. She followed her dream, and thousands, *thousands*, of children who otherwise would have ended up lost in the system are thriving today because of it . . ."

Her guests that afternoon included a woman who

had started a ranch for troubled kids, where they learned how to ride and take care of horses; a singer who had just recorded her first album, thanks to funding from Fortune; and a stay-at-home mom who had invented a line of natural bath-and-beauty products that she had sent to Fortune to try, and that Fortune was now going to carry in all her spas.

Fortune went on and on about how she was using the products herself, especially the bubble baths. "There's nothing like a good bubble bath when I need to drain away the stress of the day, or I'm searching for a new idea. I get some of my *best* ideas in the bathtub —"

"Me too!" Cleo said, feeling as if she and Fortune were chatting face-to-face.

"With Marina's Verbena-Spearmint Bubble Bath, so can you. So stay right where you are — you're not going to want to miss a second of this show!"

"Hey, babe," Dad said during the commercial, "you should send Fortune some of your Longevity Lollipops. I thought those were pretty tasty."

"Um," Cleo said, "I'm not sure that's such a good idea."

"What?" Dad said. "*You* sent her a letter."

"You can't choke on a letter. Those things almost killed me!" She and Dad laughed.

"Hey!" Mom tweaked Cleo's arm. "Don't worry. I'm not going to embarrass you by sending your idol a bunch of birdseed on sticks."

It was a really good show, as usual, even though Dad had to leave halfway through to referee a fight between the boys and stayed outside to play with them. Too quickly, Fortune was interviewing her last guest. Marina, the bubble-bath lady, had just shared about starting up her business and how listening to her customers had been super important in improving her product line.

"What you just said, girl — that's *gold*." Fortune reached out and put her hand on the woman's arm. "Pure gold!" She turned and looked at the audience. "We have to *listen* to each other. Listening is the key to doing good business, because unless you're listening to people, you won't know what they need, want, or will buy. But it's also how you make and keep your friends."

She was looking straight at the camera again. Straight at *Cleo*. "If I've learned anything, it is this: Whatever you do, listen. Listen to your customers and listen to your friends. Your friends are your most valuable assets, because while businesses come and go, your *friends*, if you treat them right, will be by your side through all the ups and downs. And believe me, my friends, if you're in business, there *will* be ups and downs."

She held up a sample of Marina's Bubble Bath Bar, a set of three bottles standing in a silver wire rack you could attach to the wall of your tub or shower. Everyone in the audience was going to get one, compliments of Fortune. People cheered and applauded. She started to say thank-yous to all her guests and to her audience and to everyone watching, her television family, but Cleo was no longer paying attention to the show.

All she could think about was Caylee. Her friend. Fortune had said, "Whatever you do, listen to your friends." Cleo had been so focused on her businesses and succeeding, she hadn't been treating Caylee as her most valuable asset. She hadn't been listening. It was time to do something about that.

Thank you, Fortune!

CHAPTER 18

Through Ups and Downs

Cleo called Caylee three times. The first two times, no one answered. The third time Ernie Junior said their mom had taken Caylee to her appointment with the shrink.

"Shrink?" Cleo asked.

"Yeah, you know. Head doctor."

Cleo was suddenly afraid. Was her best friend dying? "What's wrong with her head?"

"Nothing's wrong with her head. She's seeing a counselor, a therapist. Someone you talk to about your problems?"

The lightbulb went on. "Ohhhh . . ." She felt another stab of guilt. Her friend had needed to talk, and she hadn't been there to listen. Caylee had been *so* in need, they'd hired a professional listener. "Well, will you ask her to call me? As soon as she can?"

"Got it." Ernie Junior hung up.

Cleo waited for Caylee to call. Her family ate dinner. Caylee didn't call. Cleo put her Fortune poster back on the wall and worked on her Passion Project presentation. Caylee didn't call. She got ready for bed, and still Caylee didn't call. By nine thirty-eight, Cleo knew. Caylee wasn't going to call.

She tore a piece of paper from her memo pad, scribbled a note, and stuffed it into Barkley's Carrier Capsule. She poked her head into the hall. Mom and Dad's door was closed. The coast was clear. "Shh," she said to Barkley with her finger to her lips. She held him by his collar and tiptoed downstairs to the back door. She slipped on her flip-flops and led him outside. "Go straight there," she whispered. "No sniffing trash cans or chasing cats. No getting in trouble, like me."

Barkley's eyebrows twitched and his tongue hung out one side of his mouth. She could tell they had an understanding. He sped through the back gate and around the corner, headed for Caylee's house.

As soon as he was gone, Cleo started getting nervous. Caylee just *had* to get the message. Cleo would stand outside and wait for Barkley's return — hopefully with an "apology accepted" note from Caylee.

A moment later, the silent night air erupted with squawks and yelps. *Oh no.* It was coming from Miss Jean's. She ran back inside, grabbed her coat off its peg, and sprinted. She rounded the corner of their fence, expecting to see a fluffy ball of white feathers dangling from Barkley's mouth. Instead, she saw a gang of chickens attacking her dog!

Cleo ran up, flailing her arms. "Shoo! Shoo! Bad chickens!" Wings battered her shins as she tried to pull her dog from the center of the feathered fracas.

The porch light snapped on. Miss Jean shot out the front door in her bathrobe. She swooped in and grabbed up Big Betty, the largest one. Gloria, Alice, and Susan B quietly gathered around Miss Jean's feet, pecking at bits of gravel on her driveway.

"How did you get out, you naughty girls?" Miss Jean asked. Big Betty flapped and fluttered in her arms.

Cleo noticed the metal gate across the driveway was partway open. "Miss Jean." She pointed.

"Oh! I must not have latched it securely when I came in tonight. I'm sorry they were attacking your poor dog. You okay, Barkley?"

By the looks of him, he was fine, although he'd probably never want to have anything to do with chickens ever again. "Yeah. He'll be fine. Thanks." Cleo helped Miss Jean return the chickens to the other side of the fence. They shut the gate tight.

"What are you doing outside at this hour?" Miss Jean asked when the job was done. "Do your parents know you're out here?" She looked at Cleo suspiciously.

"I only came out because I heard Barkley.

So" — she crossed her fingers behind her back — "I'll get home now. Good night!" Cleo waved and smiled as she led Barkley by his collar toward her house, but as soon as Miss Jean was gone she turned and headed toward Caylee's. "Come on, Barkley. We've got a message to deliver."

They ran down the sidewalk to the big pink house. Cleo turned at the drive that led into the back. She stopped at the base of the balcony and looked up to see if a light was on in Caylee's bedroom. The curtains were dark. She looked around, trying to figure out the best way to get her friend's attention.

Barkley made a low grumble like he was getting ready to bark, but she clamped his mouth shut. "Not now, Barkley. I have another idea."

The balcony. All she had to do was climb onto the balcony and she'd be right beside Caylee's window.

A wooden thing made out of thin boards that crossed each other in a bunch of Xs went all the way up to the balcony. A lattice, she thought she'd heard Mrs. Ortega call it. Roses grew on it, but only as high as her waist. Lattice . . . ladder . . . they sounded kind of the same. And she was an expert ladder climber. Part mountain goat, even. As long as the wood was strong enough to hold her, she could make it to the top. No problem.

She grabbed on, found a spot for her foot, and pulled herself up. The wood felt kind of creaky, but nothing broke, so she kept going. Hand over hand. Higher, higher. Barkley yapped. She turned and shushed him and he sat, seeming to understand now was not the time.

That summer, they had pretended the balcony was the deck of a fancy cruise ship, and they were on it with their boyfriends. Cleo didn't have time for real boys, but she was fine with imaginary ones. She and Caylee had hugged themselves, closed their eyes, and made kissing sounds. They laughed until they were rolling around on the deck, holding their stomachs.

The memory almost made her laugh out loud again, but she controlled herself. She threw her leg over the railing and jumped down onto solid ground.

She looked out in triumph. Cleopatra Edison Oliver had done it again!

Barkley leaped up on the roses, then yelped and jumped back down. He must have snagged a thorn. "Stay there!" she whispered to her dog. "I'll be back in a few minutes." *Hopefully, through the back door,* she thought. Going down didn't sound as fun as going up had.

The balcony door whooshed open. Cleo spun around.

"Cleo!" Caylee stood there in her nightgown, breathing hard. "I heard you land and looked out my window. I thought someone was trying to break in!" She rushed onto the balcony and looked over the edge. "How did you get up here?"

Cleo smiled big. "Climbed, of course." Would her best friend smile back?

Caylee stared at her like she had no idea what to say.

The quiet between them made Cleo as nervous and knotted-up as standing on the end of the high dive, looking down at the super-blue water. The only way out, if you didn't want to get laughed at, was to jump. "I'm sorry," she said, making the leap. "I know I've been so focused on my businesses and Cleopatra Enterprises, and I haven't been a very good listener even though you're going through a really hard time with your dad and everything — and I've been a terrible — no, *horriful* — best friend." Her hands flew all over the place, which happened when she was talking fast. "A good business partner, maybe, but not a very good friend. And I'm sorry. I'm really, really sorry." One of her hands came to rest on Caylee's arm. She felt a pinch in her chest. "Really."

Caylee's mouth opened a little and then closed. She peered over the railing again. "Hi, Barkley." It was hard to see his black fur in the dark, but they could hear him panting, and the moon cast enough light to see his body waggling like crazy. He barked.

Caylee looked at her. She smiled. Finally. Just a little. But she smiled.

Just as quickly, her smile disappeared. "My dad is

getting married — to that girlfriend I told you about. Char*lene*." She said the name as if she were talking about pickled asparagus.

The news hit Cleo like a dodgeball to the chest. Mr. Ortega may not have been one hundred percent reliable, but she knew Caylee still loved him a whole bunch and was really hoping he would come back, in spite of everything. She had even lit a candle at her Catholic church for him. "But ... he hasn't been gone that long."

Caylee bit on her bottom lip. "I know."

Cleo leaned against the railing, her arms crossed. Why were adults always going and messing things up — and letting kids get hurt in the process? This wasn't just a bad decision, like taking a sharp knife outside or bringing a Nerf gun to school. This was tearing up a family. And families were meant to be forever. Weren't they?

"That's not even the worst of it." Caylee scowled. "His fiancée wants *me* to be a junior bridesmaid. That's why they took me shopping. To buy me a dress.

I don't even want to go to the wedding! She's, like, half his age. It's so embarrassing. Mom is really mad." She leaned against the railing and gazed in the direction of the street lamp. "Things haven't been very fun around here the past couple months."

Cleo couldn't think of anything to say. What Caylee was going through was awful. Terribly, horribly, gigantically awful. A tear popped up in the corner of Cleo's eye. She almost pushed it back down, but maybe crying because of someone else's hurt would be okay. The tear spilled over and she didn't try to hide it.

She reached out and grabbed Caylee's hand, and they stood there, saying nothing. Just feeling the cool breeze, and smelling the sweet night-blooming jasmine, and hearing Barkley sniffing around in the yard. Cleo squeezed Caylee's hand, and Caylee squeezed hers back.

"I'm sorry I hung up on you," Caylee said. "It's just, my dad seems to think money can make all this better. Like buying me a fancy camera and an iPod Touch will make me less mad."

Cleo waited to see if her friend had more to say. This listening stuff was hard, but it felt good too. Caylee seemed done. "That's okay. Besides, if I can't handle getting hung up on every once in a while, I won't make it very far in the business world." She grabbed Caylee's other hand. They faced each other. "Without friends, money doesn't mean anything, Caylee. I'm your friend . . . through the ups and downs. Promise."

"Me too."

"Shake on it?" Cleo asked. They shook hands. Then they gave each other the biggest Bug-a-Hug ever. She would never let anything get in the way of her friendship with Caylee. Nothing. Not even Cleopatra Enterprises, Inc.

Cleo wrapped her arms around herself, closed her eyes, and kissed the air. "Oh, Donovan!"

She didn't know who Donovan was. It just sounded like someone you might kiss on the deck of a fancy cruise ship.

Caylee giggled.

Cleo smooched and smooched, until Caylee was laughing for reals. Everything was okay again. "So . . . about that personalized-barrette business . . ." Cleo grinned. "What do you think about the name . . . *Caylee's Cuties?*"

Acknowledgments

Cleo is a character who has grown in my heart over several years. Thank you to the many people who either helped me bring her to life on the page or encouraged me that I could, especially my agent, Regina Brooks (it was more than just "serendipity" that caused our paths to cross); my sister-by-heart, Fina Arnold; and my partner in life and parenting, Matt Frazier. Thank you for never giving up on me.

To Arthur A. Levine, who challenged me to know the *why* behind Cleo's ladder-climbing nature—thank you for giving the feedback that gave me my second wind. Without your nurturance, Cleo would likely remain locked in my computer. Thanks to the whole Scholastic team that has so lovingly handled this story and its production: Nicholas Thomas, Emily Clement, Weslie Turner, Mary Claire Cruz, Elizabeth Krych, Bonnie Cutler, and Jennifer L. Meyer. Many authors inspire me to persevere in telling the truth through the "lie" of art; this time around, I am especially grateful to Linda Sue Park for inspiring me with her commitment to the craft.

Thanks to my young friends Lala Lopez and Ash Lawson for giving me the skinny on twenty-first-century elementary-school life, and to all the other young readers who shared their thoughts on my manuscript: Tessa Edgar, Ellie Rosic, Mia Waters, and Reese Arnold. Thank you Micheline Lopez and Stephanie Rosic for your input, as well. To my dear friends, Janet Chu and Michael Yu, and Jenny and Scott Hall, as well as my mom and dad; many thanks for your love and support over the years, and the use of your homes when our local library (aka, my writing office) was closed for renovations.

It has been especially important to me to portray the adoptive experience with sensitivity and awareness. Thank you to adoptive mom Jill Dziko (www. youradoptivefamily.com) and Jeff Carlson of Bethany in La Mirada for answering questions, and to Betty Jean Lifton, Nancy Newton Verrier, Amanda Transue-Woolston (www.thelostdaughters.com), and Angela Tucker (www.theadoptedlife.com) for writing so honestly about your personal experiences. Your stories have forever changed mine.

Finally, to Matt, Skye, and Umbria, you give me so much joy. I love being family with you.

About the Author

Sundee T. Frazier is the author of *Brendan Buckley's Universe and Everything in It,* winner of the 2008 ALA Coretta Scott King/John Steptoe New Talent Award; *Brendan Buckley's Sixth-Grade Experiment*; and *The Other Half of My Heart*. Frazier graduated from the University of Southern California with a degree in broadcast journalism in 1991 and earned her MFA in Writing for Children from Vermont College of Fine Arts in 2004. She currently lives near Seattle with her husband and two daughters.

THIS BOOK was edited by Arthur Levine and designed by Mary Claire Cruz. The text was set in Electra LT, and the display type was set in GFY Christopha. The book was printed and bound at CG Book Printers in North Mankato, Minnesota. Production was supervised by Elizabeth Krych, and manufacturing was supervised by Shannon Rice.